www.bookcrossing.com
BCID# 761-1671023

The New BLACK MASK

Number 4

EDITED BY

MATTHEW J. BRUCCOLI & RICHARD LAYMAN

A HARVEST/HBJ BOOK

HARCOURT BRACE JOVANOVICH, PUBLISHERS

SAN DIEGO   NEW YORK   LONDON

Copyright © 1986 by Harcourt Brace Jovanovich, Inc.

All rights reserved. No part of this publication may be reproduced or transmitted in any form or by any means, electronic or mechanical, including photocopy, recording, or any information storage and retrieval system, without permission in writing from the publisher.

Requests for permission to make copies of any part of the work should be mailed to: Permissions, Harcourt Brace Jovanovich, Publishers, Orlando, FL 32887.

"Loren D. Estleman: An Interview," copyright © 1985 by Loren D. Estleman. "Blond and Blue," copyright © 1986 by Loren D. Estleman. "The Sins of the Fathers," copyright © 1986 by George V. Higgins. "The Other Eye," copyright © 1981 by Edward D. Hoch. "The Scoop," copyright © 1986 by Joseph L. Koenig. "There's No Such Thing as Private Eyes," copyright © 1986 by Mark Coggins. "Pincushion," copyright © 1985 by David A. Bowman. "Psychodrama," copyright © 1986 by Mike Handley. "The Ripoff," copyright © 1985 by the Estate of Jim Thompson.

Editorial correspondence should be directed to the editors at Bruccoli Clark Publishers, Inc., 2006 Sumter Street, Columbia, SC 29201.

ISSN 0884-8963

ISBN 0-15-665483-0

Designed by G. B. D. Smith

Printed in the United States of America

First Harvest/HBJ edition 1986

A B C D E F G H I J

Contents

Loren D. Estleman: An Interview   3

Blond and Blue   13
LOREN D. ESTLEMAN

The Sins of the Fathers   50
GEORGE V. HIGGINS

The Other Eye   60
EDWARD D. HOCH

The Scoop   84
JOSEPH L. KOENIG

There's No Such Thing as Private Eyes   90
MARK COGGINS

Pincushion   123
DAVID A. BOWMAN

Psychodrama   146
MIKE HANDLEY

The Ripoff: Conclusion   155
JIM THOMPSON

Loren D. Estleman:
An Interview

Loren Estleman is a relative newcomer among hard-boiled detective novelists. His first book was published less than a decade ago. He has a background in journalism, having written for three Michigan newspapers, and he lives near Detroit, the beleaguered city Amos Walker calls home.

While he is best known to New Black Mask readers for his novels featuring either Walker or the professional hit man Peter Macklin, Mr. Estleman has also distinguished himself as a writer of Westerns, winning the Western Writers of America Golden Spur Award for his novel Aces and Eights, based on the life of Wild Bill Hickok as it is revealed during the trial of his murderer.

Critic Robin Winks has remarked that he reads Loren Estleman "for the sheer joy of seeing the phrases fall into place." A prose stylist who believes that some of the best writers in the English language take private eyes as their subjects, Mr. Estleman does not find it necessary to apologize for his material.

NBM: How long had you been writing before your first novel, *The Oklahoma Punk*, was published?
Estleman: Eight years.
NBM: So you started when you were sixteen?
Estleman: No, actually I was about fifteen.
NBM: And writing with a view toward being a professional writer?

Estleman: Oh, yeah.

NBM: Publishing?

Estleman: Yep.

NBM: Where?

Estleman: The first place I sent a short story, when I was fifteen, was *Argosy* magazine. So I had my mind on the pulp fiction market even then.

NBM: What was the attraction of the pulps?

Estleman: It seemed to be my kind of fiction. I had tried, and now and then I still try, to write one of these things that takes place entirely in someone's head, and I found that it just wasn't for me. I write stories about people who do things.

NBM: Action and adventure?

Estleman: Right.

NBM: The pulps are typically thought of as being a man's reading material.

Estleman: Yeah, to begin with, although there was a time when there were fully as many women readers as men—at least of the Westerns. Around thirty years ago men, women, and children were gobbling up Westerns by the millions.

NBM: Do you have any sense now that you are writing for a male audience?

Estleman: I am constantly interested in finding out how I am going over with a female audience. It always surprises me, and maybe it shouldn't, to learn that I have quite a large female following for the Amos Walker series. A lot of my colleagues have asked me how my Walker series does with women, because he's kind of macho as opposed to the usual modern Alan

Alda kind of hero. My answer is always the same: I seem to be going over quite well with women. What captures the female audience is Walker's type of humor. He doesn't take himself too seriously. I think that is an important ingredient in what I call the quintessential American hero, the complete revolutionary who does not take authority, others, or himself too seriously.

NBM: You have written a substantial amount of Western fiction. Why Westerns?

Estleman: I think I recognized early on that the Western is a purely American form, and it was a form that I could relate to more than, say, the European style of both living and writing. There are definite similarities between the detective form and the Western form. One of them is the revolutionary hero I talked about. The cowboy myth, if you will, the man alone, the man outside—that goes back to our own revolutionary beginning. Whether I'm writing about Amos Walker, who lives on the modern urban frontier, or a character named Page Murdock in one of my books set on the Western frontier, I'm basically writing about the same kind of person, though I am using somewhat different methods and describing different forms of civilization. Nevertheless, it's the same person underneath it all. The idea of the lone revolutionary-type hero has produced a purely American form. Too often we overlook in our fiction Ned Buntline, Prentiss Ingraham, Owen Wister, Jack Schaeffer, Louis L'Amour, and some of the more sophisticated Western writers. You can draw a straight line from the

Street & Smith Buffalo Bill stories and Ned Buntline stories right to Street & Smith's pulps of the twenties and thirties and forties and then to today's paperback novels. That type of story is beginning to make itself known in the hardcovers now.

NBM: There's a classic affinity between the Western and mystery fiction.

Estleman: There are definite differences too. The mystery is more complex in the way it deals with nature and a bit more cerebral because of it. I don't mean puzzles of the Agatha Christie type. Detectives depend on their minds a little bit more than their physical reactions.

NBM: The setting of detective fiction is certainly more complex.

Estleman: The settings are basically different, and yet somehow the same too. Both are set in a kind of a gray-area frontier where the only real law is the law that a man makes for himself.

NBM: If my count is right, your fourteenth book will be published in spring 1986.

Estleman: Actually my twenty-second. If you ask me about that, I will say that I remember writing every one of those twenty-two books, but I don't remember writing twenty-two books.

NBM: You have series novels with at least three publishers. For Houghton Mifflin you do the Amos Walker mysteries; for Mysterious Press you do the Macklin series; and for Doubleday you do the Westerns. Have you ever written under a pseudonym?

Estleman: I never have. Never felt the urge to. I

never really trusted it in the people that I read because I always felt that what they wrote under a pseudonym was something that they didn't put their heart and soul into. I always thought that if I ever did write under a pseudonym, subconsciously I would not make it as good as if I were putting my own name on it. I'm much more comfortable with my own name, because knowing that my reputation is going to depend forever on that book, I'm going to make it as good as I can.

NBM: Is there one of your series characters that makes your heart beat a little faster, that you anticipate writing about with a little more excitement?

Estleman: Yes. When I'm writing a Western I'd rather be writing a mystery, and vice versa. It always works that way. That's why we're paid. But you're always thinking ahead to the next project wishing you were doing something else, because when you get to the nuts and bolts, it's not as romantic as it was when you first had the idea. They all make my heart beat faster, though, when the writing's going well. I may be more comfortable in the Western form. I can't really tell you why. Maybe it's because it's a little bit freer, and I can depend on those reactions a little bit more. And you can use a little bit more action and not feel as if you're just greasing a story up. That's how things were done out West; they were men of action. But I certainly wouldn't give up the mystery for anything. Any time I begin to contemplate a new Walker book, it's like seeing an old friend. As long as that continues, I'm going to continue to do it. If I ever find myself writing a Walker book just to write a Walker book, that would be the time to quit that series and go on to something else. It has to be enjoyable for me or it's not going to be enjoyable for my readers.

NBM: Why do you write short stories? With your writing schedule they would seem to be a distraction and not worth your time.

Estleman: I enjoy them; they're a challenge. They are certainly a change of pace when I have finished a long project like a novel. I enjoy writing short stories. And yet, probably when you talk about intensive work, a short story is exceedingly more difficult to write than a novel. It's kind of like making love on an elevator; you have to know where you're going from the beginning. You have to nail your character down in a couple of lines and move on from there—keep it in constant movement. It's been said that those who can't write poetry write short stories, and those who can't write short stories write novels. I don't know about the poetry part because it's been twenty, twenty-five years since I've tried poetry. But I do know that short stories are a challenge.

NBM: Do you ever worry, as Hemingway might put it, that the juices might dry up?

Estleman: Not consciously, but certainly when I'm between books and more than a couple of weeks—well, let's be honest—when more than about two days pass, I start to climb the walls. There's always that little niggling doubt somewhere in the back of my mind that maybe I've lost it and can't do it anymore, and I have to glue myself to the typewriter and get back in the harness and prove to myself that I can. That may be a valuable asset.

NBM: In nine years of book publishing you've established yourself in the first rank of writers in two genres, if you also count Westerns, both of which are becoming more and more respectable.

Estleman: Very good people have been working in the Western field, and I fear that the average reader hears so much about Louis L'Amour that he'll pick up a L'Amour book and think that this is as good as it gets. L'Amour writes well, not as well as he used to, but he still writes well. But there are people who are doing classic American literature in that form who are not as well known.

NBM: Aside from talent, which is obvious, to what do you attribute the success you have enjoyed in a relatively short professional career? A lot of people, presumably even talented people, have books that they can't get published.

Estleman: Sure. Those stories are all over the place. Both world and American literature would be immeasurably richer if a lot of books that never were published had gotten to the right people. I think that many fine, fine writers have been and are being overlooked. I know a few myself. I think the real danger that we face now is the mania for categorization. The average publisher is afraid to touch a book that doesn't fall into an acceptable pigeonhole. They don't know how to present and how to handle books otherwise. I think that's going to be a problem for a while. I had a realistic approach from the beginning. I knew that the kind of writing I wanted to do would be the kind that could be popular. And, also, I thought that I could maintain my integrity, and I feel that I have by doing the best that I am able to do. At the same time I'm lucky enough that the kind of writing I'm most comfortable with is the kind that tends to be the most popular. Yet I've never really gone with the trends. If I see a trend developing, I almost immediately head in the opposite direction. That's how it was with Amos Walker. When I started Amos Walker, there were no other major private detective figures out there except Bob Parker's Spenser, and when I first started doing Westerns, they were at their nadir both critically and popularly. I guess there was a certain amount of luck there. After my first book, I landed an excellent agent who I still have and who can speed things up immeasurably because he knows to whom to send a book. I've had a series of very good editors along the way who have well understood what it is I'm trying to do and have known how much to take part and when to back off and defer to me. I may be more comfortable and more knowledgeable as a result of these circumstances, and that is a valuable asset. At the same time, I look around and I see extremely good, Nobel prize–quality writers who are just not being published.

NBM: You said that the writers whose works have had the most profound influence on your own writing are Edgar Allan Poe, Jack London, and Raymond Chandler. How big a factor is the writing of others in your work? Or to put it differently, how dependent are you as a writer on literary history?

Estleman: I think every writer is definitely dependent on those who have gone before us. Both on their mistakes and on the trail that they've blazed. I can't pinpoint any one person who has been the greatest influence on me. They have all been influences to some degree. And that's not a bad thing. It's a good place to start as long as you can move on from there and advance the cause that these other writers started. I read a great deal, and I make it a practice not to read writers who do not themselves read. We read for the same reason a baseball player looks at a videotape of another player in action. Certainly a pitcher does it to see how his opponent works and to see if he can better it. You also read to know what's going on around you; and it's good for the soul. Two things can make you sit down and write. One is reading a book that is really bad, thinking I could do much better; the second is reading a book that's very good. It makes that old fear work up, and you think maybe I better get back in the harness here and establish myself.

NBM: Television seems hungry now for detective series, especially hard-boiled detective series. These shows haven't been in vogue for about fifteen years. Why the interest all of a sudden?

Estleman: It would have to do with our continuing interest in crime. Crime is something that happens to people you've never heard of, except when it happens to your next-door neighbor, or to people in your family, or to you and me. As long as we are potential victims, the interest in crime fiction is going to continue—certainly in detective fiction in which the criminal gets caught, because it's something you don't see too much in everyday life. It's definitely going to continue to grow as time goes by. The reason private detectives themselves are of interest now is this American revolutionary concept. At the moment, I think people are sick and tired of police, and they want to see something a little less structured than police procedure. They want to see basically ordinary men of an extraordinary makeup doing things the police can't because of the Bill of Rights, the Supreme Court, and the inertia of modern American law enforcement.

NBM: So you don't think that detective fiction or detective material is in danger of being oversold, as Donald Westlake has suggested?

Estleman: Probably not. I don't think that it can be oversold. I think that there's going to be a lot of bad detective fiction written; there always has. And along the way there's going to be a lot of good fiction. But as far as being oversold, I don't see that happening.

NBM: You're now thirty-three years old. Do you anticipate with tranquility another thirty years of writing fiction?

Estleman: Oh, yes. That's what I've been doing so far, and that's what I've always wanted to do. I don't see that changing. I can't tap-dance or sing. So I think I'll stick with the talent I have. I do hope that I'm going to continue to get better, and I hope never to sell out.

Blond and Blue
LOREN D. ESTLEMAN

"The following story is based on an actual incident, which at last word was still unresolved," Loren Estleman writes about "Blond and Blue."

Since the appearance of his story "Bloody July" in NBM 1, Mr. Estleman has been a busy writer. In October 1985, Mysterious Press published his second novel about professional hit man Peter Macklin, Roses Are Dead; *in November, Doubleday published* Gun Man, *"a serious study of an authentic Western gunfighter"; and in March, Houghton Mifflin will publish a new Amos Walker novel,* Every Brilliant Eye.

ERNEST KRELL's aversion to windows was a legend in the investigation business. It was a trademark, like his tie clasp made from a piece of shrapnel the army surgeons had pried out of his hip in Seoul and his passion for black suits with discreet patterns to break up their severity. During his seventeen years with the Secret Service he had spent so many public hours warning presidential candidates' wives away from windows that when it came time to open his own detective agency he dug into his wife's inheritance to throw up a building that didn't have any. Narrow vertical slits set eight feet apart let light into a black marble edifice that looked like a blank domino from anywhere along the Detroit River.

A receptionist with blue stones in her ears and that silver complexion that comes free with fluorescent lights took my hat and left me alone in Krell's office, a bowling alley of a room carpeted in black and brown and containing oak-and-leather chairs and an antique desk in front of a huge Miró landscape, lots of blues and reds, to make up for the lack of a window. The walls were painted two shades of cinnamon, darker on the desk side of the office to keep the customers where they belonged. A lot of framed citations, Krell's license, and a square black-on-white sign reading "RELIANCE—Courtesy, Efficiency, Confidentiality" took care of the bare spots.

There were no ashtrays, so I took a seat near a potted fern and lit a cigarette, tipping my ashes into the pot. After five puffs the man himself came in through a side door and scowled at the curling smoke and then at me and said, "There's no smoking in this building."

"I didn't see any signs," I said.

"You don't see any ashtrays either." He ran a hand under the edge of the desk. A second later, the silver-skinned receptionist came in carrying an ashtray used just for putting out smokes, and I did that. I couldn't decide if it was the way he had pushed the button or if I just had the look of a guy that would light up in the boss's office. When she left carrying my squashed butt, the man extended his hand and I rose to take it. His grip was cool and firm and as personal as a haberdasher's smile.

"Good to meet you, Walker. I don't think I've had the pleasure."

"This is the first time I've gotten any higher than the fourth floor," I said.

Krell chuckled meaninglessly. He was six three and two hundred pounds, a large pale man with black hair that looked dyed and wrinkles around his eyes and mouth from years of squinting into the sun looking for riflemen on rooftops. It was orange today, orange stripes on his black suit and jaunty orange sunbursts on his silk tie to pick it up. It softened the overall effect of his person like a bright bow tied to a buffalo's tail made you forget he was standing on your foot. The famous tie clasp was in place.

He waved me into one of the chairs but remained upright at parade rest with his hands folded behind him. "I spent last night reading the files on the cases you assisted us with," he said. "Despite the fact that you're anything but the Reliance type"—his gaze lit on my polyester suit—"you show a certain efficiency I admire. Also you spend more time and effort on each client than a Reliance operative could afford."

"You can do that when they only come into your office one at a time," I volunteered.

"Yes." He let the word melt on his tongue, then

pressed on. "The reason I asked you to come down today, we have a client who might best benefit from your rather unorthodox method. A delicate case and a highly emotional one. Frankly, I'd have referred her to another agency had she not come recommended by one of our most valued clients."

"She?"

"You'll meet her in a moment. It's a missing persons situation, which I believe is your specialty. Her son's been kidnapped."

"That's the FBI's specialty."

"Only in cases where ransom is demanded. On the statutes it's abduction, which would make it a police matter except that her ex-husband is the suspected culprit. The authorities consider that a domestic problem and approach it accordingly."

"Meaning it gets spiked along with the butcher's wife who threw a side of pork at her husband," I said. "How old is the boy?"

"Seven." He quarter-turned toward the desk and drew a typewritten sheet from a folder lying open on top. "Blond and blue, about four feet tall leaning to pudgy, last seen April third wearing a blue-and-white-striped T-shirt, red corduroy shorts, and dirty white sneakers. Answers to Tommy. One minute he was playing with a toy truck in the front yard of his mother's home in Austin, Texas, and the next there was just the truck. Neighbor thought he saw him on the passenger's side of a low red sports car going around the corner. The ex-husband owns a red Corvette."

"That's April third this year?" I asked. It was now early May.

"I know it's a long time. She's been to all the authorities here and in Texas."

"Why here?"

"A relative of the mother is sure she saw the father at the Tel-Twelve Mall in Southfield three weeks ago. She flew in right after. Staying at the relative's place."

"What makes it too hot to touch?"

He stroked the edge of the sheet with a meaty thumb, making a noise like a cricket. "The ex-husband is an executive with a finance corporation I sometimes do business with. If it gets out I'm investigating one of its employees—"

"Last stop for the money train," I finished. "What's to investigate? She should've gone back to court to start, put the sheriffs on his neck."

"His neck is gone and so is he. He took a leave of absence from his company, closed out his apartment in Austin and vanished, boy and all. He probably had all his bags packed in the Corvette's trunk when he picked up Tommy and just kept driving. It's all here." He put the sheet back inside the folder and handed the works to me.

It ran just five pages, triple-spaced and written in Reliance's terse, patented preliminary-report language, but on plain paper without the distinctive letterhead. Very little of it was for me. The ex-husband's name was Frank Corcoran. He was a house investments counselor for Great Western Loans and Credit, with branch offices in seventeen cities west of the Mississippi. There were two numbers to call for information there. The name and number of the witness who had seen his car at the time of the boy's disappearance were there too, along with the 'Vette's serial number and license plate. It was long gone by now or the cops in Austin or Detroit would have had it in on a BOL weeks ago. I folded the report into quarters anyway and put it in a pocket and gave back the empty folder. "Can I talk to the mother?"

"Of course. She's in the other office."

I followed him through the side door into a room separate from the one where the receptionist sat, a chamber half the size of Krell's, decorated in muted warm colors and containing a row of chairs with circular backs, like the room in a funeral home where the family receives visitors. "Charlotte Corcoran, Amos Walker," said Krell.

The woman seated on the end chair raised a sunken face to look at me. Her jaw was too long to be pretty, but it had been an attractive face before she started losing weight, the bones sculpted, not sharp like now, the forehead high and broad instead of jutting and hollow at the sides. The little bit of lipstick she wore might have been painted on the corpse in that same funeral home. Her hair was blond and tied back loosely with wisps of gray springing loose around her ears. Her dress was just a dress, and her bare angular legs ended in bony feet thrust into low-heeled shoes a size too large for her. She was smoking a cigarette with a white filter tip. I peered through the haze at Krell, who moved a shoulder and then flipped a wall switch that started a fan humming somewhere in the woodwork. The smoke stirred and began twisting toward a remote corner of the ceiling. I got out a Winston and sent some of my own after it.

"My boy Tommy turned seven last week," Charlotte Corcoran told the wall across from her. "It's the first birthday I missed."

Her speech had an east Texas twang. I twirled another chair to face hers and sat down. The connecting door clicked shut discreetly behind Krell. It was the only noise he made exiting. "Tell me about your husband," I said.

She snicked some ash into a tray on the chair next to her and looked at me. Seeing me now. "I could call him a monster. I'd be lying. Before this the worst thing he did was to call a half hour before supper to say he was working late. He did that a lot; it's part of why I divorced him. That's old news. I want my son back."

"What'd the police in Austin say?"

"They acted concerned until I told them he'd been kidnapped by his father. Then they lost interest. They said they'd put Tommy's picture on the bulletin board in every precinct, and maybe they did. They didn't give it to the newspapers or TV the way they do when a child's just plain missing. I got the same swirl of no action from the police here. Kidnapping's okay between relatives, I guess." She spat smoke.

"Skipping state lines should've landed it in the feds' lap," I said.

"I called the Houston office of the FBI. They were

polite. They test high on polite. They said they'd get it on the wire. I never saw any of them."

"So far as you know."

It was lost on her. She mashed out her butt, leaving some lipstick smeared on the end. "I spent plenty of time at Police Headquarters here and back home," she said. "They showed me the door nice as you please, but they showed me the door. They wouldn't tell me what they'd found out."

"That should have told you right there."

Her expression changed. "Can you find them, Mr.— I've forgotten."

"Walker," I said. "A lot rests on whether they're still here. And if they were ever here to begin with."

"Frank was. My cousin Millie doesn't make mistakes."

"That's Millicent Arnold, the relative you're staying with?" She nodded. "I'll need a picture of Tommy and one of Mr. Corcoran."

"This should do it." From her purse she drew a five-by-seven bureau shot and gave it to me. "I took it last summer on a trip to Corpus Christi. Tommy's grown several inches since. But his face hasn't changed."

I looked at a man with dark curly hair and a towheaded boy standing in swim trunks on a yellow beach with blue ocean behind them. "His father didn't get that build lifting telephone receivers."

"He worked out at a gym near his office. He was a member."

I pocketed the photograph next to the Reliance report and stood up. "I'll be in touch."

"I'll be in."

Krell was on the intercom to his receptionist when I reentered his office. I waited until he finished making his lunch reservation, then:

"How much of a boost can I expect from Reliance on this one?"

"You already have it," he said. "The situation is—"

"Delicate, yeah. I'll take my full fee, then. Three days to start."

"What happened to professional courtesy?"

"It went out of style, same as the amateur kind. What about it? You're soaking her five bills per day now."

"Four fifty." He adjusted his tie clasp. "I'll have Mrs. Marble draw you a check."

"Your receptionist has access to company funds?"

"She's proven herself worthy of my trust."

I didn't say it. My bank balance was stuck to the sidewalk as it was.

The report had Mrs. Corcoran in contact with a Sergeant Grandy in General Service, missing persons detail. I deposited half of the Reliance check at my bank, hanging on to the rest for expenses, and drove down to Police Headquarters, where a uniform escorted me to a pasteboard desk with a bald head behind it. Grandy had an egg-salad sandwich in one hand and a styrofoam cup of coffee in the other and was using a blank arrest form for a place mat. He wore a checked sport coat and a moustache healthy enough to have sucked all the hair from his scalp.

"Corcoran, yeah," he said, after reading my card and hearing my business. "It's in the works. You got to realize it don't get the same priority as a little boy lost. I mean, somebody's feeding him."

"Turn anything yet?"

"We got the boy's picture and the father's description out."

"That's what you've done. What've you got?"

He flicked a piece of egg salad off his lapel. "What I got is two Grosse Pointe runaways to chase down and a four-year-old girl missing from an apartment on Watson I'll be handing to Homicide soon as she turns up jammed in a culvert somewhere. I don't need part-time heat too."

We were getting started early. I set fire to some tobacco. "Who's your lieutenant?"

"Winkle. Only he's out sick."

"Sergeant Grandy, if I spent an hour here, would I walk out any smarter than I was when I came in?"

"Probably not."

"Okay. I just wondered if you were an exception."

I was out of there before he got it.

On the ground floor I used a pay telephone to call the Federal Building and explained my problem to the woman who answered at the FBI.

"That would be Special Agent Roseman, Interstate Flight," she said. "But he's on another line."

I said I'd wait. She put me on hold. I watched a couple of prowl-car cops sweating in their winter uniforms by the Coke machine. After five minutes the woman came back on. "Mr. Roseman will be tied up for a while. Would you like to call back?"

I said yeah and hung up. Out on Beaubien the sidewalks were throwing back the first real warmth of spring. I rolled down the window on the driver's side and breathed auto exhaust all the way to my office building. You have to celebrate it somehow.

The window in my thinking parlor was stuck shut. I strained a disk heaving it open a crack to smell the sweet sun-spread pavement three stories down. Then I sat down behind the desk—real wood, no longer in style but not yet antique—and tried the FBI again. Roseman was out to lunch. I left my number and got out the Reliance report and dialed one of two numbers for the firm where Frank Corcoran worked in Austin.

"Great Western." Another woman. They own the telephone wires.

I gave her my name and calling. "I'm trying to reach Frank Corcoran. It's about an inheritance."

"I'm sorry, Mr. Corcoran is on indefinite leave."

"Where can I reach him?"

"I'm sorry."

I thanked her anyway and worked the plunger. I wasn't disappointed. It's basic to try the knob before you break out the lockpicks. I used the other number, and this time I got a man.

"Arnold Wilson, president of Thornbraugh Electronics in Chicago," I said. Thornbraugh Transmissions on Livernois put out the advertising calendar tacked to the wall across from my desk. "We're building a new plant in Springfield and Frank Corcoran advised me to call Great Western for financing. Is he in?"

"What did you say your name was?" I repeated it. "One moment."

I had enough time to pluck out a cigarette before he came back on the line. "Are you the private investigator who spoke to my partner's secretary about Mr. Corcoran a few moments ago?" His tone had lost at least three layers of silk.

"What's the matter," I said, "you don't have any walls in that place?"

I was talking to myself. As I lowered the dead receiver I could hear the computers gossiping among themselves, trashing my credit rating. The laugh was on them; I didn't have one.

My next trip was through the yellow pages. There were at least fifty public gymnasiums listed within a half hour of downtown Detroit, including Southfield, any one of which would suit Corcoran's obsession with a healthy body. We all have our white whales. I made a list of the bigger, cleaner places. It was still long. Just thinking about it made my feet throb.

I tried the number of the place where Charlotte Corcoran was staying in Southfield. A breathy female voice answered, not hers.

"Millicent Arnold?"

"Yes. Mr. Walker? Charlotte told me she spoke with you earlier. She's napping now. Shall I wake her?"

"That's okay. It's you I want to talk to. About the man you saw who looked like Frank Corcoran."

"It was Frank. I spent a week in their home in Austin last year, and I know what he looks like."

"Where did you see him at the mall? In what store?"

"He was coming out of the sporting goods place. I was across the corridor. I almost called to him over the crowd, but then I remembered. I thought about following him, see where he went, but by the time I made up my mind he was lost in the crush. I went into the store and found the clerk who had waited on him. He'd paid cash for what he bought, didn't leave a name or address."

"What'd he buy, barbell weights?" Maybe he was working out at home and I could forget the gyms.

"No. Something else. Sweats, I think. Yes, a new sweat suit. Does that help?"

"My feet will give you a different answer. But yeah. Thanks, Miss Arnold."

"Call me Millie. Everyone does."

I believed her. It was the voice.

After saying good-bye I scowled at the list, then raised my little electronic paging device from among the flotsam in the top drawer of the desk and called my answering service to test the batteries. They were deader than the Anthony dollar. I said I'd call in for messages and locked up.

The office directly below mine was being used that month by a studio photographer, five foot one and three hundred pounds with a Marlboro butt screwed into the middle of a face full of stubble. I went through the open door just as he finished brushing down the cowlick of a gap-toothed ten-year-old in a white shirt buttoned to the neck and blue jeans as stiff as aluminum siding and waddled around behind the camera, jowls swinging. "Smile, you little—" he said, squeezing the bulb on the last part. White light bleached the boy's face and the sky blue backdrop behind.

When the kid had gone, following the spots in front of his eyes, I handed the photographer the picture Charlotte Corcoran had given me of her ex-husband and their son. "How much to make a negative from this and run off twenty-five prints?" I asked.

He held the shot close enough to his face to set it afire if his stub had been burning. "Eighty-seven fifty."

"How much for just fifteen?"

"Eighty-seven fifty."

"Must be the overhead." I was looking at a rope of cobwebs as thick as my wrist hammocking from the ceiling.

"No, you just look like someone that wants it tomorrow."

"Early." I gave him two fifties and he changed them from a cigar box on a table cluttered with lenses and film tubes and wrote me out a receipt.

I used his telephone to call my service. There were no messages. I tried the Federal Building again. Special Agent Roseman had come in and gone out and wasn't expected back that day. He had the right idea. I went home and cooked a foil-wrapped tray for supper and watched the news and a TV movie and went to bed.

I was pulling a tail.

Leaving the diner I let fix my breakfast those mornings I can't face a frying pan, I watched a brown Chrysler pull out of the little parking area behind me in the rearview mirror. Three turns later it was still with me. I made a few more turns to make sure and then nicked the red light crossing John R. The Chrysler tried to do the same but had to brake when a Roadway van trundled through the intersection laying down horn.

I was still thinking about it when I squeezed into the visitors' lot outside Police Headquarters. My next alimony payment wasn't due for a month, and I hadn't anything to do with the Sicilian boys' betterment league all year.

Sergeant Grandy had a worried-looking black woman in a ratty squirrel coat in the customer's chair and was clunking out a missing persons report with two fingers on a typewriter that came over with Father Marquette. I asked him if Lieutenant Winkle was in today.

"What for?" He mouthed each letter as he typed.

"Corcoran, same as yesterday."

"Go ahead and talk to him. I had a full head of hair before people started climbing over it."

I followed his thumb to where a slim black man in striped shirt-sleeves and a plain brown tie was filling a china mug at the coffee maker. He wore a modest Afro and gray-tinted glasses. I gave him a card.

"I've been hired by Charlotte Corcoran to look for her ex-husband and their boy Tommy," I said. "The sergeant wasn't much help."

"Told you to walk off a dock, right?" His eyes might have twinkled over the top of the mug, but you can never be sure about cops' eyes.

"Words to that effect."

"Grandy's gone as high as he's going in my detail," he said. "No diplomacy. You have some identification besides a card?"

I showed him the chintzy pastel-colored ID the state hands out. He reached into a pocket and flipped forty cents into a tray full of coins next to the coffee maker. "Let's go into the cave."

We entered an office made of linoleum and amber pebbled glass, closing the door. He set down his mug, tugged at his trousers to protect the crease, and sat on the only clear corner of his desk. Then he pulled over his telephone and dialed a number.

"Hello, Miss Arnold? This is Lieutenant Winkle in General Service. . . . Millie, right. Is Mrs. Corcoran in? Thank you." Pause. "Mrs. Corcoran? No, I'm sorry, there's nothing new. Reason I called, I've got a private investigator here named Walker says he's working for you. . . . Okay, thanks. Just wanted to confirm it."

He hung up and looked at me. "Sorry. Department policy."

"I'm unoffendable," I said. "How many telephone numbers you keep in your head at any given time?"

"Last month I forgot my mother's birthday." He drowned his quiet smile in coffee. "We have nothing in the Corcoran case."

"Nothing as in nothing, or nothing you can do anything with?"

"Nothing as in zip. We run on coffee and nicotine here. When we get a box full of scraps we can hand over to the feds, we don't waste time trying to assemble them ourselves. The FBI computer drew a blank on Corcoran."

"Not unusual if he doesn't have priors."

"It gets better. Because of the exodus from Michigan to Texas over the past couple of years, a lot of local firms have been dealing with finance companies out there. So when it landed back in our lap, we fed Great Western Loans and Credit into the department machine. Still nothing on Corcoran, because only the officers are on file. But the printout said the corporation invests heavily in government projects. As investments counselor, Frank Corcoran should have shown up on that FBI report. He'd have had to have been screened one time or another."

"Some kind of cover-up?"

"You tell me. The word's lost a lot of its impact in recent years."

I opened a fresh pack of Winstons. "So why keep Mrs. Corcoran in the dark?"

"Don't worry. It's not rubbing off on us," he said. "We're just holding her at arm's length till we get some answers back from channels. These things take time. Computer time, which is measured in Christmases."

"So why tell me?"

He smiled the quiet smile. "When Sergeant Grandy gave me your card I did some asking around the building. If you were a bulldog you'd have what the novelists call 'acquisitive teeth.' Quickest way to get rid of you guys is to throw you some truth."

"I appreciate it, Lieutenant." I rose and offered him my hand. He didn't give it back as hastily as some cops have. "Oh, what would you know about a brown Chrysler that was shadowing me a little while ago?"

"It wasn't one of mine," he said. "I'm lucky to get a blue-and-white when I want to go in with the band."

I grasped the doorknob. "Thanks again. I guess you're feeling better."

"Than what? Oh, yesterday. I called in sick to watch my kid pitch. He walked six batters in a row."

I grinned and left. That's the thing I hate most about cops. Find one that stands for everything you don't like about them and then you draw one that's human.

The job stank, all right. It stank indoors and it stank on the street and it stank in the car all the way to my building. I had the window closed this trip: the air was damp and the sky was throwing fingers whether to rain or snow. Michigan. But it wouldn't have smelled any better with the window down.

The pictures came out good, anyway. It must be nice to be in a business where if they don't you can trace the problem to a bad filter or dirt in the chemicals, something definite and impersonal that you can ditch and replace with something better. I left the fat photographer developing nude shots for a customer on Adult Row on Woodward and went upstairs.

I lock the waiting room overnight. I was about to use the key when the door swung inward and a young black party in faded overalls and a Pistons warm-up jacket grinned at me. He had a mouth built for grinning, wide as a Buick with door-to-door teeth and a thin moustache squared off like a bracket to make it seem even wider. "You're late, trooper," he said. "Let's you come in and we'll get started."

"Thanks, I'll come back," I said, and backpedaled into something hard. The wall was closer this morning. A hand curled inside the back of my collar and jerked my suit coat down to my elbows, straining the button and pinning my arms behind me.

Teeth drew a finger smelling of marijuana down my cheek. Then he balled his fist and rapped the side of my chin hard enough to make my own teeth snap together.

"Let's you come in, trooper. Unless you'd rather wake up smiling at yourself from your bedside table every morning."

I kicked him in the crotch.

He said, "Hee!" and hugged himself. Meanwhile I threw myself forward, popping the button and stripping out of my coat. My left arm was still tangled in the sleeve lining when I pivoted on my left foot and swung my right fist into a face eight inches higher than mine. I felt the jar to my shoulder. I was still gripping the keys in that hand.

The guy I hit let go of the coat to drag the back of a huge hand under his nose and looked at the blood. Then he took hold of my shirt collar from the front to steady me and cocked his other fist, taking aim.

"Easy, Del. We ain't supposed to bust him." Teeth's voice was a croak.

Del lowered his fist but kept his grip on my collar. He was almost seven feet tall, very black, and had artificially straightened hair combed into a high pompadour and sprayed hard as a brick. In place of a jacket he wore a full-length overcoat that barely reached his hips, over a sweatshirt that left his navel and flat hairy belly exposed.

Behind me Teeth said, "Del don't like to talk. He's got him a cleft palate. It don't get in his way at all. Now you want to come in, talk?"

I used what air Del had left me to agree. He let go and we went inside. In front of the door to my private office Teeth relieved me of my keys, unlocked it, and stood aside while his partner shoved me on through. Teeth glanced at the lock on his way in.

"Dead bolt, yeah. Looks new. You need one on the other door too."

He circled the room as he spoke and stopped in front of me. I was ready and got my hip out just as he kicked. I staggered sideways. Del caught me.

"That's no way to treat a client, trooper," Teeth said. "It gets around, pretty soon you ain't got no business."

"Client?" I shook off the giant's steadying hand. My leg tingled.

Teeth reached into the slash pocket of his Pistons jacket and brought out a roll of crisp bills, riffling them under my nose. "Hundreds, trooper. Fifty of them in this little bunch. Go on, heft it. Ain't no heavier'n a roll of quarters, but, my oh my, how many more smiles she draws."

He held it out while I got my coat right side in. Finally his arm got tired and he let it drop. I said, "You came in hard for paying customers. What do I have to forget?"

"We want someone to forget something, we go to a politician," he said. "Twenty-five hundred of this pays to look for somebody. The other twenty-five comes when the somebody gets found."

"Somebody being?" Knowing the answer.

"Same guy you're after now. Frank Corcoran."

"That standard for someone who's already looking for him for a lot less?"

"There's a little more to it," he said.

"Thought there might be."

"You find him, you tell us first. Ahead of his wife."

"Then?"

"Then you don't tell her."

"I guess I don't ask why."

His grin creaked. "You're smart, trooper. Too smart for poor."

"I'll need a number," I said.

"We call you." He held up the bills. "We talking?"

"Let's drink over it." I pushed past him around the desk and tugged at the handle on the deep drawer. Teeth's other hand moved and five inches of pointed steel flicked out of his fist. "Just a Scotch bottle," I said.

He leaned over the corner to see down into the drawer. I grabbed a handful of his hair and bounced his forehead off the desk. The switchblade went flying. Del, standing in front of the desk, made a growling sound in his chest and lurched forward. I yanked open the top drawer and fired my Smith & Wesson .38 without taking it out. The bullet smashed through the front panel and buried itself in the wall next to the door. It didn't come within a foot of hitting the big man. But he stopped. I raised the gun and backed to the window.

"A name," I said. "Whose money?"

Teeth rubbed his forehead, where a purple bruise was spreading under the brown. He stooped to pick up the currency from the floor and stood riffling it against his palm. His smile was a shadow of a ghost of what it had been. "No names today, trooper. I'm fresh out of names."

I said, "It works this way. You tell me the name, I don't shoot you."

"You don't shoot. Desks and walls, maybe. Not people. It's why you're broke, and it's why I get to walk around with somebody else's five long ones on account of it's what I drop on gas for my three Cadillacs."

"What about a Chrysler?"

"I pay my dentist in Chryslers," he said. "So long, trooper. Maybe I see you. Maybe you don't see me first. Oh." He got my keys out of his slash pocket and flipped them onto the desk. "We're splitting, Del."

Del looked around, spotted my framed original *Casablanca* poster hanging on the wall over the bullet hole, and swung his fist. Glass sprayed. Then he turned around and crunched out behind his partner, speckling my carpet with blood from his lacerated fingers.

The telephone rang while I was cleaning the revolver. When I got my claws unhooked from the ceiling I lifted the receiver. It was Lieutenant Winkle. He wanted to see me at Headquarters.

"Something?" I asked.

"Everything," he said. "Don't stop for cigarettes on the way."

I reloaded, hunted up my holster, and clipped the works to my belt. No one came to investigate the shot. The neighborhood had fallen that far.

On Beaubien I left the gun in the car to clear the metal detectors inside. Heading there I walked past a brown Chrysler parked in the visitors' lot. There was no one inside and the doors were locked.

The lieutenant let me into his office, where two men in dark suits were seated in mismatched chairs. One had a head full of crisp gray hair and black-rimmed glasses astride a nose that had been broken sometime in the distant past. The other was younger and looked like Jack Kennedy with a close-trimmed black beard. They stank federal.

"Eric Stendahl and Robert LeJohn." Winkle introduced them in the same order. "They're with the Justice Department."

"We met," I said. "Sort of."

Stendahl nodded. He might have smiled. "I thought you'd made us. I should have let Bob drive; he's harder to shake behind a wheel. But even an old eagle likes to test his wings now and then." The smile died. "We're here to ask you to stop looking for Frank Corcoran."

I lit a Winston. "If I say no?"

"Then we'll tell you. We have influence with the state police, who issued your license."

"I'll get a hearing. They'll have to tell me why."

"That won't be necessary," he said. "Corcoran was the inside man in an elaborate scheme to bilk Great Western Loans and Credit out of six hundred thousand dollars in loans to a nonexistent oil venture in Mexico. He was apprehended and agreed to turn state's evidence against his accomplices in return for a new identity and relocation for his protection. You're familiar with the alias program, I believe."

"I ran into it once." I looked at Winkle. "You knew?"

"Not until they came in here this morning after you left," he said. "They've had Mrs. Corcoran under surveillance. That's how they got on to you. It also explains why Washington turned its back on this one."

I added some ash to the fine mulch on the linoleum floor. "Not too bright, relocating him in an area where his wife's cousin lives."

Stendahl said, "We didn't know about that, but it

certainly would have clinched our other objections. He spent his childhood here and had a fixation about the place. The people behind the swindle travel in wide circles; we couldn't chance his being spotted. Bob here was escorting Corcoran to the East Coast. He disappeared during the plane change at Metro Airport. We're still looking for him."

"It's a big club," I said. "We ought to have a secret handshake. What about Corcoran's son?"

LeJohn spoke up. "That's how he lost me. The boy was along. He had to go to the bathroom, and he didn't want anyone but his father in with him. I went into the bookstore for a magazine. When I got back to the men's room, it was empty."

"The old bathroom trick. Tell me, did Corcoran ever happen to mention that the boy was in his mother's custody and that you were acting as accomplices in his abduction?"

"He seemed happy enough," said LeJohn, glaring. "Excited about the trip."

His partner laid manicured nails on his arm, calming him. To me: "It was a condition of Corcoran's testimony that the boy go with him to his new life. Legally, our compliance is indefensible. Morally—well, his evidence is expected to put some important felons behind bars."

"Yeah." I tipped some smoke out my nostrils. "I guess you got too busy to clue in Mrs. Corcoran."

"That was an oversight. We'll correct it while we're here."

"What did you mean when you said it was a big

club?" LeJohn pressed me. "Who else is looking for Corcoran?"

I replayed the scene in my office. Lieutenant Winkle grunted. "Monroe Boyd and Little Delbert Riddle," he said. "I had one or both of them in here half a dozen times when I was with Criminal Intelligence. Extortion, suspicion of murder. Nothing stuck. So they're jobbing themselves out now. I'll put out a pickup on them if you want to press charges."

"They'd be out the door before you finished the paperwork. I'll just tack the price of a new old desk and a picture frame on to the expense sheet. The bullet hole's good for business."

"How'd they know you were working for Mrs. Corcoran?" Stendahl asked.

"The same way you did, maybe. Only they were better at it."

He rose. "We'll need whatever you've got on them in your files, Lieutenant. Walker, you're out of it."

"Can I report to Mrs. Corcoran?"

"Yes. Yes, please do. It will save us some time. You've been very cooperative."

He extended his hand. I went on crushing out my cigarette in the ashtray on Winkle's desk until he got tired and lowered it. Then I left.

Millicent Arnold owned a condominium off Twelve Mile Road, within sight of the glass-and-steel skyscrapers of the Southfield Civic Center sticking up above the predominantly horizontal suburb like new teeth in an old mouth. A slim brunette with a pageboy haircut answered the bell wearing a pink angora sweater over black harem pants and gold sandals with high heels on her bare feet. Charlotte Corcoran might have looked like her before she had lost too much weight.

"Amos Walker? Yes, you are. My God, you look like a private eye. Come in."

I kept my mouth zipped at that one and walked past her into a living room paved with orange shag and furnished in green plush and glass. It should have looked like hell. I decided it was Millie Arnold standing in it that made it work. She hung my hat on an ornamental peg near the door.

"Charlotte's putting herself together. She was asleep when you called."

"She seems to sleep a lot."

"Her doctor in Austin prescribed a mild sedative. It's almost the only thing that's gotten her through this past month. You said you had some news." She indicated the sofa.

I took it. It was like sitting on a sponge. "The story hangs some lefts and rights," I said.

She sat next to me, trapping her hands between her knees. She wasn't wearing a ring. "My cousin and I are close," she said. "More like sisters. You can speak freely."

"I didn't mean that, although it was coming. I just don't want to have to tell it twice. I didn't like it when I heard it."

"That bad, huh?"

I said nothing. She tucked her feet under her and propped an elbow on the back of the sofa and her cheek in her hand. "I'm curious about something. I recommended Reliance to Charlotte. She came back with you."

"The case came down my street. Krell said she was referred to him by one of his cash customers."

She nodded. "Kester Clothiers on Lahser. I'm a buyer. I typed Charlotte's letter of reference on their stationery. The chain retains Reliance for security, employee theft and like that."

"I guess the hours are good."

"I'm off this week. We're between seasons." She paused. "You know, you're sort of attractive."

I was looking at her again when Charlotte Corcoran came in. She had on a maroon robe over a blue nightgown, rich material that bagged on her and made her wrists and ankles look even bonier than they were. Backless slippers. When she saw me her step quickened. "You found them? Is Tommy all right?"

I took a deep breath and sat her down in a green plush chair with tassels on the arms and told it.

"Wow," said Millie after a long silence.

I was watching her cousin. She remained motionless for a moment, then fumbled cigarettes and a book of matches out of her robe pocket. She tried to strike a match, said "Damn!" and threw the book on the floor. I picked it up and struck one and held the flame for her. She drew in a lungful and blew a plume at the ceiling. "The bastard," she said. "No wonder he never had time for me. He was too busy making himself rich."

"You didn't know about his testifying?" I asked.

"He came through with his child support on time. That's all I heard from him. It explains why he never came by for his weekends with Tommy." She looked at me. "Is my son in danger?"

"He is if he's with his father. Boyd and Riddle didn't look like lovers of children. But the feds are on it."

"Is this the same federal government that endowed a study to find out why convicts want to escape prison?"

"Someone caught it on a bad day," I said.

"How much to go on with the investigation, Mr. Walker?"

"Nothing, Mrs. Corcoran. I just wanted to hear you say it."

She smiled then, a little.

"What progress have you made?" asked Millie.

"I'm chasing a lead now. If it gets any slimmer it won't be a lead at all. But it beats reading bumps." I got the package of prints out of my coat pocket, separated the original of Corcoran and Tommy from the others, and gave it back to Mrs. Corcoran. "I've got twenty-five more now, and at least that many places to show them. When I run out I'll try something else."

She looked at the picture. Seeing only one person in it. Then she put it in her robe pocket. "I think you're a good man, Mr. Walker."

Millie Arnold saw me to the door. "She's right, you know," she said, when I had it open. "You are good." Attractive, too.

There was a gymnasium right around the corner on Greenfield. No one I talked to there recognized either of the faces in the picture, but I left it with the manager anyway along with my card and tried the next place on my list. I had them grouped by area with Southfield at the top. I hit two places in Birmingham, one in Clawson, then swung west and worked my way home in a loop through Farmington and Livonia. A jock in Redford Township with muscles on his T-shirt thought Corcoran looked familiar but couldn't finger him.

"There's fifty dollars in it for you when you do," I said. He flexed his trapezius and said he'd work on it.

I'd missed lunch, so I stopped in Detroit for an early supper, hit a few more places downtown, and went back to the office to read my mail and call my service for messages. I had none, and the mail was all bills and junk. I locked up and went home. That night I dreamed I was Johnny Appleseed, but instead of trees every seed I threw sprang up grinning Monroe Boyds and hulking Delbert Riddles.

My fat photographer neighbor greeted me in the foyer of my building the next morning. He was chewing on what looked like the same Marlboro butt, and he hadn't been standing any closer to his razor than usual.

GRAZ
Grazer, Gigi Levangie.
Seven deadlies : a cautionary tale /
3208903868541.3   bib   Grazer, Gigi Levangie.
Adult Fiction

HERR
Herron, Jaclynn, auth
Rewriting Marguerite : a novel /
3208904137144.9   bib   Herron, Jaclynn, author.
Adult Fiction

KAWA
Kawakami, Mieko, 197
Heaven /
3208904598832.1   bib   Kawakami, Mieko, 1976-
Adult Fiction

LE
The Gangster we are all looking for /
Le, Thi Diem Thuy, 197.

Landscaping
742-16710215

Black mask
761-16710213

"Some noise yesterday," he said. "Starting a range up there or what?"

"No, I shot a shutterbug for asking too many questions." I passed him on the stairs, no small feat.

I entered my office with my gun drawn, felt stupid when I found it empty, then saw the shattered glass from the poster frame and felt a little better. I swept it up and called my service. I had a message.

"Walker?" asked a male voice at the number left for me. "Tunk Herman, remember?"

"The guy in Redford," I said.

"Yeah. That fifty still good?"

"What've you got?"

"I couldn't stop thinking about that dude in the picture, so I went through the records of members. Thought maybe his name would jump out at me if I heard it, you know? Well, it did. James Muldoon. He's a weekender. I don't see him usually because I don't work weekends, except that one time. I got an address for him."

I drew a pencil out of the cup on my desk. It shook a little.

It was spring now and no argument. The air had a fresh damp smell and the sun felt warm on my back as I leaned on the open-air telephone booth, or maybe it was my disposition coming through from inside. Charlotte Corcoran answered on the eighth ring. Her voice sounded foggy.

"Walker, Mrs. Corcoran," I said. "Come get your son."

"What did you say? I took a pill a little while ago. It sounded—"

"It wasn't the pill. I'm looking at him now. Blond and blue, about four feet—"

The questions came fast, tumbling all over one another, too tangled to pull apart. I held the receiver away from my ear and waited. Down the block, on the other side of Pembroke, a little boy in blue overalls with a bright yellow mop was bouncing a ball off the wall of a two-story white frame house that went back forever. While I was watching, the front door came open and a dark-haired man beckoned him inside. Corcoran's physique was less impressive in street clothes.

"Tommy's fine," I said, when his mother wound down. "Meet me here." I gave her the address. "Put Millie on and I'll give her directions."

"Millie's out shopping. I don't have a car."

"Take a cab."

"Cab?"

"Forget it. You've got too much of that stuff in your pipes to come out alone. I'll pick you up in twenty minutes."

It was all of that. The road crews were at work, and everyone who had a car and no job was out enjoying the season. I left the engine running in front of the brick complex and bounced up the wrought-iron steps to where Millie's door stood open. I rapped and went inside. Charlotte Corcoran was sitting on the sofa in her robe and nightgown.

"That's out of style for the street this year," I said. "Get into something motherly."

"Plenty of time for that."

I felt my face get tired at the sound of the voice behind me. I turned around slowly. Millie Arnold was standing on the blind side of the door in a white summer dress with a red belt around her trim waist and a brown .32 Colt automatic in her right hand pointing at me.

"You don't look surprised." She nudged the door shut with the toe of a red pump.

"It was there," I said, raising my hands. "It just needed a kick. I had to wonder how Boyd and Riddle got on to me so fast. They couldn't have been following Mrs. Corcoran without Stendahl and LeJohn knowing. Someone had to tell them."

"It goes back farther than that. I made two calls to Texas after spotting Frank at the mall. The first was to his old partners. I can't tell you how much they appreciated it. If I did, I'd be in trouble with the IRS. Then I called Charlotte. Throw the gun down on the rug, Mr. Walker. It made an ugly dent in my sofa when you were here yesterday."

I unholstered the .38 slowly. It hit the shag halfway between us with a thump. "Then, when Mrs. Corcoran arrived, you talked her into hiring the biggest investigative firm you knew. You figured to let them do the work of finding Corcoran. It probably meant a discount on Boyd and Riddle's fee."

"It also guaranteed me a bonus when Frank got

dead," she said. "Krell giving the case to you threw me, but it worked out just fine. When I got back from shopping and Charlotte gave me the good news, I just couldn't wait to call our mutual friends and share it."

"My cousin," said Mrs. Corcoran.

Millie showed her teeth. Very white and a little sharp. "You married a hundred-thou-a-year executive. I'd have settled for that. But if it wasn't enough for him, why should what I make be enough for me? I met his little playmates that time I visited you in Austin. I had a hunch there was money to be made. When I called, they told me just how and why."

"What happens to us?" I asked.

"You'll both stay here with me until that phone rings. It'll be Boyd giving me thumbs up. I'll have to lock you in the bathroom when I leave, but you'll find a way out soon enough. You can have the condo, Charlotte. It isn't paid for."

"The boy had nothing to do with Corcoran's scam," I said. "You're putting him in front of the guns too."

"Rich kid. What do I owe him?"

"They won't hurt Tommy." Mrs. Corcoran got up.

"Sit down." The gun jerked.

But she was moving. I threw my arm in front of her. She knocked it aside and charged. Millie squeezed the trigger. It clicked. Her cousin was all over her then, kicking and shrieking and clawing at her eyes. It was interesting to see. Millie was healthier, but she was standing between a mother and her child. When the gun came up to slap the side of Mrs. Corcoran's head, I tipped the odds, reversing ends on the Smith & Wesson I'd scooped up from the rug and tapping Millie behind the ear. Her knees gave then and she trickled through her cousin's grasp and puddled on the floor.

I reached down and pulled her eyelids. "She's good for an hour," I said. "Call nine one one. Give them the address on Pembroke."

While she was doing that, breathing heavily, I picked up the automatic and ran back the action. Millie had forgotten to rack a cartridge into the chamber.

Approaching Pembroke, we heard shots.

I jammed my heel down on the accelerator and we rounded the corner doing fifty. Charlotte Corcoran, still in her robe, gripped the door handle to stay out of my lap. Her profile was sharp against the window, thrust forward like a mother hawk's.

There was no sign of the police. As we entered Corcoran/Muldoon's block, something flashed in an open upstairs window, followed closely by a hard flat bang. A much louder shot answered it from the front yard. There a huge black figure in an overcoat too short for him crouched behind a lilac bush beside the driveway. His .44 magnum was as long as my thigh but looked like a kid's water pistol in his great fist.

"Hang on!" I spun the wheel hard and floored the pedal.

The Olds's engine roared and we bumped over the

curb, diagonaling across the lawn. Del Riddle straightened at the noise and turned, bringing the magnum around with him. I saw his mouth open wide and then his body filled the windshield and I felt the impact. We bucked up over the porch stoop and suddenly the world was a deafening place of tearing wood and exploding glass. The car stopped then, although my foot was still pasted to the floor with the accelerator pedal underneath and the engine continued to whine. The rear wheels spun shrilly. I cut the ignition. A piece of glass fell somewhere with a clank.

I looked at my passenger. She was slumped down in the seat with her knees against the dash. "All right?"

"I think so." She lowered her knees.

"Stay here."

The door didn't want to open. I shoved hard and it squawked against the buckled fender. I climbed out behind the Smith & Wesson in my right hand. I was in a living room with broken glass on the carpet and pieces of shredded siding slung over the chairs and sofa. Riddle lay spreadeagled on his face across the car's hood and windshield, groaning. His legs dangled like broken straws in front of the smashed grille.

"Ditch the piece, trooper."

My eyes were still adjusting to the dim light indoors. I focused on Monroe Boyd baring his teeth in front of a hallway running to the back of the house. He had one arm around Tommy Corcoran's chest under the arms, holding him kicking above the floor. His other hand had a switchblade in it with the point pressing the boy's jugular.

"Tommy!" Charlotte Corcoran had gotten out on the passenger's side. She took a step and stopped. Boyd bettered his grip.

"Mommy," said the boy.

"What about it, trooper? Seven or seventy, they all bleed the same."

I relaxed my hold on the gun.

A shot slammed the walls and a blue hole appeared under Boyd's left eye. He let go of Tommy and lay down. Twitched once.

I looked up at Frank Corcoran crouched at the top of the staircase to the second story. His arm was stretched out full length with his gun in it, leaking smoke. He glanced at Tommy. "I told you to stay upstairs with me."

"I left my ball here." The boy pouted, then spotted Boyd's body. "Funny man."

Mrs. Corcoran flew forward and knelt to throw her arms around her son. Corcoran saw her for the first time, said "Charlotte?" and looked at me. The gun came around.

"Stop waving that thing," his ex-wife said, hugging Tommy. "He's with me."

Corcoran hesitated, then lowered the weapon. He surveyed the damage. "What do I tell the rental agent?"

I heard the sirens then.

The Sins of the Fathers

GEORGE V. HIGGINS

George V. Higgins is recognized as having the best ear for speech of any writer now practicing his craft in America. Praise for his dialogue implies that he is simply an accurate transcriber; but Mr. Higgins's use of dialogue utilizes a sophisticated narrative technique in which authorial exposition is eliminated and the omniscient writer is replaced by the omniscient reader. George V. Higgins's The Friends of Eddie Coyle *has been selected as one of the twenty novels in the British Book Marketing Council's Authors USA promotion. His thirteenth novel,* Imposters, *will be published by Holt, Rinehart and Winston in the spring.*

"I AM TELLING YOU right now," Norbert Johnson said, "that you would not believe, that no sane person would believe, what I go through with this guy." He wore a gray T-shirt that said "Property New England Patriots" on the front, encircling a Patriots logo of a colonial soldier preparing to throw a football. He sat behind the old wooden desk in the range master's office at the Watertown Sportsman's Club in the basement of the old Franklin Pierce School. The first floor had been converted to a YMCA, and there was a basketball game in progress over Norbert's head. The vibration made the big green pipes in the basement shake on their hanging rods, dislodging droplets of condensed moisture onto Norbert's desk. To his right, behind the steel safety door with the pane of safety glass at eye level in the center, the Wellesley Annie Oakleys enjoyed their weekly hour shooting at cardboard targets, the dull, thin concussions of their S&W .38s, 9 mm.'s, and Beretta .25s coughing through the padded paneling.

"You're gonna," Shanahan said, nodding toward the top of the desk where Norbert had a chromed Colt .45 automatic apart, "you're gonna get that thing all screwed up, you get it wet like this."

Johnson looked down irritably at the gun. "Oh, I could give a shit," he said. "You know whose gun this is? This is Lieutenant Foster's personal sidearm, that's whose gun it is. And you know the last time Lieutenant Foster personally cleaned his personal sidearm? Lemme give you a clue, all right? Eisenhower was president."

"Oh, come on," Shanahan said. "Foster's only about forty. Can't be that long ago."

"Oh, bullshit," Johnson said. "You'n' me're thirty-five. You're forgetting: time goes by. Don't matter who you are. Charlie Foster's fifty-five. Fifty-four at least."

"He can't be," Shanahan said. "He's in beautiful shape if he is, and besides, even if he is, that'd only make him, what, about . . ."

"About twenny years old when Ike was president," Johnson said. "Which happens to be what he was. And sure, he's in beautiful shape. Wouldn't you be in beautiful shape, you never did a fuckin' thing? Course you would, you jerk. Guy doesn't even clean his own goddamned gun, for Christ sake. Naturally he's got the skin of Elizabeth Taylor anna look of a man half his age. Heaviest thing the guy's lifted since he turned eighteen's a sandwich. A sandwich he paid for, of course—Lieutenant Foster takes no graft. He's got integrity. Plus balls the size of an elephant's, but that's another thing."

"Well," Shanahan said, nodding toward the dismantled .45, "then I assume he's paying you, I mean. For cleaning his gun for him."

"Oh," Norbert said, "sure he is. He's paying me ten bucks. Which when I get it, I will treat you to a beer. Which I hope you're not very thirsty for, right about now, because I have done this job before, for Lieutenant Foster. I have done it lots of times, for the same ten bucks. And you know how many ten bucks I have seen for doing it? 'None' would be a real good guess. You couldn't miss with that."

"He doesn't pay you?" Shanahan said. "I wouldn't take that from the old son of a bitch. I'd tell him he can take his gun and stick it up his ass."

"I think you would," Johnson said. "I really think you would."

"Well, I would," Shanahan said. "I've done it before."

"And you can do that," Johnson said, "because you don't mind, he tells you: 'Aw right, Shanahan, you prick, go patrol the lumberyard all night, and see how you like that.' That's why you can do that."

"Well," Shanahan said, "that's all right, if he does that. I don't give a shit. I'd rather count the fuckin' boards'n kiss Foster's big fat ass." He snickered. "I got at least one ball, Norbert. That's more'n you can say."

"No, it's not," Norbert said. "I got both my balls. The problem I have got is this: my father's got both his."

"Your father's retired," Shanahan said. "There's no way Foster can get at your father. Your father is retired. He don't, Foster can't, put your father inna lumberyard. What's this shit you're giving me, your father, all that crap."

"My father," Johnson said, "my fucking goddamned father. I'm telling you, it's like I said. You just would not believe it. You know how him and my mother, they don't get along?"

"What difference does it make, Norbert?" Shanahan said. "Them two're, they're at least divorced, we started onna force. And that was sixteen years ago, I first meet your old man. He wasn't living with her then. He was off by himself."

"Right," Johnson said. "He had the pad down Inman, down in Inman Square, took the trolley car to work. And Foster was the sergeant then. Fuckin' prodigy. And Foster knows Gerard don't live in the city, like the rules require. And Foster is all over him, got the needle out. So you know who cleaned Foster's gun, until Gerard retires? Gerard cleans Foster's gun, is who. Gerard cleans Foster's gun. Gerard picks up his laundry for him. *Gerard shines his brass.* Gerard's his personal servant, right? Gerard's his fuckin' slave. Because if Gerard's not his slave, Gerard is out of work." He paused. "Besides, Leo Sullivan was chief, and you know how Leo was. Knight of Malta, all that shit, Communion every day. One of his cops left his wife, he'd better be a Protestant, or kiss his ass goodbye. You think Foster reams you out, with the lumberyard? It's nothing, boy, compared to Leo. Leo was a holy terror. You could ask anyone.

"Now," Johnson said, "Gerard retires. Comes under the heart bill. Hits the old blood pressure jackpot onna fuckin' annual physical. 'Clean your locker out, Gerard. Hate to do this to you, chum. You know how it is. Got to have our finest fit. No invalids in here.' I thought he was gonna have a goddamned attack from laughing, he got home and calls me up after he gets the news. 'I did it, Norbert,' he keeps saying, 'I outlasted them. I took their crap for all those years, and now I'm getting out. Forty-eight years old, full pay, I got the shooting range for days and nights all to myself. I tell you, kid, stick by that job. That job will stick by you.'

"The very next day," Johnson said, "the very next fucking goddamned *day*, I go in as usual, the afternoon, and I'm down my locker getting my stuff on, and who's this standing next to me but Sergeant Mac-Intosh. Good old Sergeant MacIntosh. Mack wouldn't kiss a goat's ass unless the goat had seniority. Then he would lick the thing and tell the goat it tasted good, and could he have some more. 'Lieutenant Foster wants to see you, his office,' Mack tells me. And then he goes limping off like he's got a load in his pants, and I finished getting dressed and report. And Foster looks me up and down and says: 'Well, Patrolman Johnson, hear your old man got the pink slip. Hear old Gerard's left the force.' And I say, I hem and haw 'cause I know they hate each other, I say: 'Yessir, he has.' And he gives me this nasty-looking grin, and he says. "Well, Norbert, then I guess that just leaves you.'

"Now," Johnson said, "I'm stupid, all right? I admit it. I don't know a lot. All those years that my father's been kissing Foster's ass and trying, stay out of his way, doing his errands and all of that shit, I thought it was personal. But it wasn't personal, see? Maybe was in the beginning, Foster's looking around for some way he can ride my old man, and he thinks: 'Hey, I'll make the bastard do my fuckin' errands for me.' But then, after all those years, the reason for it, you know, didn't matter any more. Now it was just a matter, Foster gettin' his fuckin' errands done for him. He was *used* to it. So, he hears Gerard is gettin' through, and he thinks: 'Holy shit. I'm gonna have to pick up my own stuff, the cleaners. I'm gonna have to, when my car needs the inspection sticker, I'm gonna have to take it down the garage myself. What the hell do I do now?' And then he thinks: 'I know what I'll do now. I'll think up some way, get Gerard's kid to do my shit.' And that is what he did."

"I don't understand," Shanahan said. "Your father, okay, he didn't live in the city. But you, shit, you live there. You live right down on Congreve Street. What's he got on you?"

"Well," Johnson said, "it's very simple, once you think about it. See, my old man, when Gerard and my mother split up there, it's not because my old man, he's lost interest in gettin' his ashes hauled, all right? He always was a fuckin' rooster, so he says at least, struttin' around and braggin' all the time he's maybe not very big but his dick is always hard. He used to have this habit where he'd whip it out, you know? He'd bet you, he'd say all these wild things, and I guess he must've been able to get it up whenever he wanted. I guess he must've been able to do that, because whenever he'd bet, down the bar or something with the boys, he always won. So, him and my mother split up, which finally gives her a vacation, I guess, and he starts. . . . What he does is start going the massage parlors, all right? That is what he does.

"Now," Johnson said, "I'm a reasonable man. I been around some. I don't mean I'm your basic man the fuckin' world or any of that shit there, but I've been a few places and I had my share of pussy and I know what's goin' on, all right? I know what's goin' on. But I don't care how much you know, where you been, what you seen, or what you've done, it's still embarrassing when your old man's hangin' out the massage parlors. It's fuckin' embarrassing's what it is, and there's no two ways about it.

"So," Johnson said, "naturally old Foster, the guy knows everything, naturally he finds out one way or the other what my old man's doing over there in Cambridge three, four times a week. Or having done to him'd be more like it, actually. And the son of a bitch when my father retires, he calls me in his office and like I say he's got this mean grin on his face, and he tells me, he gives me his personal gun and he tells me he wants it cleaned. And naturally I look at him like he just must've lost his goddamned mind, and I give him some lip. 'Oh, good for you, Lieutenant,' I say. 'Take care of your weapon, and your weapon'll take care of you.' And he says: 'Clean it.' And I say: 'Fuck you I will. Clean it yourself.' And he says: 'I'm not finished. Also: 'fore you come in tomorrow, pick up my suits down at Prestige,' and he gives me a twenny-dollar bill and a claim check, 'and when you get through there, stop off down at Bradlee's and pick up a couple of them smoke alarms they got on sale this week.' And he throws another twenny onna desk. And I look at him. I can't believe this shit. And I say: 'The fuck you think you are, handin' me this crap? I haven't got enough time, get my own errands done. The fuck makes you think I should run around for you?'

" 'Glad you asked,' he says, and he whips open the desk drawer and pulls out this set of pictures, maybe half a dozen eight-by-tens, and they're all pictures of my father, goin' in and coming out, the Persian Delight.

'Now lemme tell you a few things, Junior Johnson,' Foster says. 'The first thing is that the young lady's name is Dawn and he always asks for her. Which he does because when she was a little kid, her mummy didn't take good care of her teeth, which means the ones she's got in her mouth now she can take out, and apparently this broad can suck a golf ball through a hundred feet of garden hose. And the second thing is that Dawn has got a brother who is doing time in Concord on a Middlesex sentence the Cambridge DA got for him, and she wants him paroled. Which the DA is willing to do if Dawn tells the grand jury about all the things that the Persian Delight does for people. Except that the DA needs a john, all right? Someone that will get up onna stand and corroborate what Dawn says. Which is a hard item to find, since most of the guys that go in there don't care to testify about what they go in there for.

" 'So,' he says," Johnson said, " 'the question I have got for you is this: Are you gonna do what I want done? Or am I gonna tell my good friend the DA I know a guy who goes there and he'll have to testify or I'll yank his pension rights. You want some time to think about it? Or are you gonna be sensible, and do like I say?' "

Johnson shrugged. "So I'm cleaning his gun," Johnson said.

"The son of a bitch," Shanahan said.

"My father, you mean," Johnson said.

"Your father I don't," Shanahan said. "I mean that fuckin' Foster."

Johnson shook his head. "You got to, Jake," he said, "you got to find some way, you don't just get all cranked off at somebody before you think things through. It ain't Foster that's my problem, all right? It's my fuckin' father, that's my problem here. I get in here today about fifteen minutes late, which I got stuck in traffic and there's no way I can help that, and I got Foster's fuckin' gun in my kit because it's that time again, and you know what I get from him? From Gerard, I mean? 'Where the hell've you been, you selfish little bastard? Don't you know that Dawn's got clients? She's got her appointments? You're supposed to be on time, you little bastard, you.' And back and forth, and this and that, I tell you: it was awful."

"And you're taking this," Shanahan said.

"Well," Johnson said, "I don't have a whole lotta goddamned choice, you know? I got the old man, and I got fucking Foster, and I got the fucking job onna force, and I got to keep all of them. You look at the whole thing serious, and there isn't one of them I can get rid of, if I'm sensible. Which I am, because somebody sure should be."

"I don't believe this," Shanahan said. "I don't believe what I am hearing. What you're telling me."

"See?" Johnson said. "That's what I told you. That's exactly what I said."

The Other Eye

EDWARD D. HOCH

Edward D. Hoch was born in Rochester, New York, in 1930 and resides there now. A former advertising executive, he sold his first story in 1955. Since then he has published more than seven hundred short stories as well as novels. A former president of the Mystery Writers of America, he was awarded an Edgar for "The Oblong Room."

Mr. Hoch comments that "this story is probably my favorite of the thirteen stories I've written about private eye Al Darlan. I wrote it in 1981 for a contest sponsored by the Third International Congress of Crime Writers in Stockholm, Sweden. . . . Although it didn't win one of the three top prizes, it was the first of the runner-up winners to be named." "The Other Eye" was published in a British collection, but this marks its first American publication.

THE DAY STARTED POORLY with the arrival of the morning mail. The only first-class letter was a reminder from my landlord that the office rent was overdue. I was wondering what to do about it when Mike Trapper walked through the partly open doorway.

"Pardon me, are you Al Darlan?"

He was tall and blond and young—young enough to

be my son. "That's me," I admitted. "Al Darlan Investigations, just like the sign says. What can I do for you?"

"I'm looking for a job. I want to learn the private detective business."

"Afraid I'm not taking on any help this week, kid."

He sat down without being asked, and slipped off his sports jacket. The office was muggy with late July heat. "Look, I'm just out of college, and I've got a little money saved up. I don't want a job. I'm looking for a small business I can buy into."

"Buy into?" I frowned and thought of the letter from my landlord. "What's your name, kid?"

"Mike Trapper." He stuck out his hand and I shook it. "I've had four years at Cornell, including a lot of pre-law courses. I was going to enter law school like my dad, but I decided I couldn't take another couple years of classes and books. I'm twenty-two and I want to get started with my life."

"What makes you think you want to be a private investigator?"

"I figure it's the closest thing to the law. You do a lot of work for lawyers, don't you?"

"Occasionally," I admitted. "But there's nothing glamorous about this work. If you've been stuffing your head with books about California private eyes, let me tell you—"

"I know."

"It's not even messy divorce cases anymore. Nobody needs a private detective to win a divorce case in this state. It's staking out department stores to catch some employee going out the back door with a camera or a couple of shirts. It's chasing after some kid who's been kidnapped by its father after the mother won custody in a divorce case. It's maybe even doing an illegal telephone tap for some guy who doesn't trust his business partner."

"I know," he repeated.

"And you still want to do it?"

"Sure."

"I've got a small operation here."

"That's why I picked it. I can't afford to start big."

"There's not even a secretary right now. I had to let her go."

"How much would it cost me to buy in for, say, a third of the business?"

"I'd have to think about that. I can't rush into this."

"Ten thousand is all the money I could afford to invest."

"Where'd a college kid manage to save ten thousand?"

"Here and there. My dad said he'd stake me to part of it."

I sighed and scratched my head. "Look, Mike, I've got to level with you. There's not even enough business here to keep one person busy. The one-man private agency is a thing of the past. I outlived my profession. Go down to one of the big outfits and start out working on insurance cases. They always need smart young kids like you."

"I don't want that, Mr. Darlan. I want a place like this."

"There's no liquor in the desk drawer. And I keep my gun in that big iron safe most of the time. I just turned fifty years old—"

"Ten thousand dollars, Mr. Darlan. Will it buy me a third of the business?"

I looked over at the dirty window and the dusty bookshelves and wondered what the hell I was letting myself in for. Was I just going to pull this kid into bankruptcy with me?

"Maybe a quarter of the business," I said quietly.

And so it happened.

A week later he moved in, and I had a sign painter change the lettering on the door to read *Darlan & Trapper, Investigations.*

"Looks good, doesn't it?" he asked, seeing it for the first time.

"Not bad," I admitted. "I used some of your money to spruce up the office a bit, and to get you a good used desk. And I took out a small announcement ad on the business page of the morning newspaper. That might bring us in something."

He looked over the desk and tried the chair. "I guess I'll need a typewriter too, for letters and reports."

I was about to suggest he could use mine, but that didn't seem right on his first day. "I'll rent you one for a month, till we can find a good one to buy."

"Swell."

"Your dad coming by to see the office?" I asked casually.

"Uh, no—not right away. He wanted to, but I thought he should wait awhile till we get settled."

"That's probably best," I agreed.

I set to work on the telephone trying to drum up business then, because I couldn't have the two of us sitting around doing nothing all day. I got lucky on the third phone call, to one of the big agencies. Some of their people were on vacation, and they were farming out a few routine insurance jobs. I told them my new partner Mike Trapper would be right over.

He was gone all afternoon and hadn't returned by the time I locked up the office a little before six. At the bar around the corner where I often stopped for a drink, I ran into Sergeant O'Keefe from Headquarters. We'd been casual friends for years, and as he slipped on to the stool next to me he said, "I hear you got yourself a partner, Al."

"Yeah, kid just out of college. Wants to learn the business. I was down yesterday and got him a license."

"Who in hell'd want to be a private eye these days? Does he think he'll get rich?"

"Family's got money. Maybe the pay doesn't matter to him."

"What's his name?"

I took a sip of Scotch. "Mike Trapper. You'll probably see a request for a gun permit come through for him."

O'Keefe patted my shoulder. "Hell, Al, maybe it's a good thing. Maybe it's like having a son to carry on the business."

"Yeah."

The next morning I had to wind up some business on a shoplifting case. After that, on my way down to the office, I stopped by a gun shop and picked out a five-shot Smith & Wesson caliber .38 Terrier. I told the clerk to put it aside, that we'd be in with the permit in a day or two. I figured if the kid invested ten grand in my business I could afford to buy him his first gun.

When I reached the office I was surprised to see the door standing open. Mike Trapper was inside at his desk, over in the opposite corner from mine. But he wasn't alone. A tall white-haired man occupied the visitor's chair. Mike jumped up as I entered.

"Al, we have a client! This is Craig Winton; Al Darlan. I met Mr. Winton over at the insurance office. He has a perplexing problem and he thinks we can help him."

Craig Winton's handshake was firm, and his eyes reflected a shrewd intelligence I'd often noticed in successful middle-aged businessmen. "A pleasure to meet you, Mr. Darlan. Your young partner here impressed me at the office this morning. I decided your firm might be able to help me with an annoying situation." He glanced around at the big single room as he spoke, and I feared for a moment that the kid had oversold us.

"We're hoping to move to larger quarters soon," I explained. "My secretary is on vacation, but when she returns we'll be moving to a suite of offices on the fifth floor."

His cool eyes studied me and he smiled slightly. "I

chose your agency because I wanted a small outfit. Our insurance firm deals routinely with the larger agencies in fraud investigations. I know those people, and I don't want them involved in my personal affairs. It wouldn't be good for our future business relationship."

"I understand completely," I said. "What's the nature of your problem, Mr. Winton?"

"I explained it to Mike on the way over. Someone seems to be impersonating me. It started about three months ago when I flew to Las Vegas for a convention. The clerk at the hotel insisted I'd arrived a day earlier, stayed one night, and then checked out that morning. I considered it a foolish mix-up, and didn't think too much about it. But a month later there was a similar occurrence. This imposter or double actually showed up at a meeting where I was to speak. Several people saw him, but he disappeared just before the time of my arrival."

"Have you reported this to the police?" I asked.

"There's been nothing to report. The imposter has committed no crime, and in fact has shown no attempt to harm me in any way. And yet—"

"There must have been more recent instances," I said. "The last one you mentioned was two months ago. What caused you to act now?"

"I suppose it's that the appearances of this phantom double are becoming more personal all the time. Last month, while I was out of the office for lunch, he actually walked past my secretary, entered my private office, and remained there for five minutes. When I returned from lunch she asked me what I'd come back for. Believe me, I was prepared to call the police that time! But nothing on my desk had been disturbed, nothing was missing."

"What did you tell your secretary?"

"I insisted it hadn't been me. She dropped the subject, probably thinking I'd had too many luncheon martinis."

"And the latest appearance?"

Craig Winton gave me another of his tired smiles. "Yes, there was one just yesterday. You may have guessed that's why I'm acting today. My wife saw him in our garage yesterday morning, after I'd left for the office. She thought it was me."

"Did he speak to her?"

"Yes. He muttered something about forgetting his briefcase. Then he left before she could get a good look at him. She phoned me later at the office and asked if I was all right."

"And you told her about this double?"

"I told her the whole story last night for the first time. She insisted I go to the police with it. We finally compromised, and I agreed to hire a private detective."

Mike Trapper shook his head. "Weird, isn't it, Al?"

"Strange," I agreed. "And just a bit menacing. You're aware of the pattern in all this, of course."

"Pattern?" the kid asked, but Craig Winton gave a little nod. He knew what I meant.

"Yes. The first time he appeared, the double was seen only by a hotel clerk who didn't know me. The second time he was seen by some casual business associates who knew me slightly. The third time my secretary saw him. And the fourth time my wife saw him."

"It's leading up to the grand finale," I said. "The next time you'll see him."

"I read a story in college about a doppelganger," Mike said. "That's German for a sort of ghostly double. When someone sees his own doppelganger it's supposed to kill him."

I picked up a pad and started making some notes. "Do you have a weak heart, Mr. Winton?"

He shook his head. "Strong as an ox. I have a checkup every year."

"So we can assume no one's trying to scare you to death. What about a twin? Do you have any brothers?"

"Only a sister living out west. You can be sure there's no secret twin hiding someplace."

I turned to the kid. "You want to work on this, Mike?"

"I sure do!"

"All right." I pulled a figure out of the air and told Winton how much we charged per day, plus expenses. He didn't bat an eye, and I wished I'd made it higher. "I want you to give Mike here a schedule of everything you'll be doing for the next week. Every business meeting, every luncheon or dinner engagement, even social events with your wife. Mike's going to be one step ahead of you, and sometimes one step behind you. Meanwhile, I'll do some investigating on my own."

Craig Winton got to his feet and shook hands once more. "I believe I'm in competent hands. You've taken a load off my mind already."

"We'll want to speak with Mrs. Winton, and possibly with your secretary as well."

"Go right ahead."

After he'd gone, Mike Trapper was beaming with pleasure. "I got us a client, Al! The first real client for Darlan and Trapper!"

"That was good work. I couldn't have done better myself." I meant it, yet I was puzzled as to why a man like Winton would have chosen a kid he'd never met before. I'd listened to his explanation about wanting a small agency and it made sense. And yet—

"You don't really think it's a ghost, do you? A doppelganger sort of thing?"

"I stopped believing in ghosts a long time ago. For one thing, they've got no money to pay my bills."

In the morning we drove out to the suburbs and visited Rina Winton. Somehow I wasn't surprised when she turned out to be a curly-haired blond at least twenty years younger than her husband. Divorce and remarriage to a younger woman seemed to go with success in the executive suite these days.

"What can you tell us about this man who impersonated your husband, Mrs. Winton?"

Though I asked the question, her eyes were all over Mike, like she was undressing him while we talked. "Frankly, Mr. Darlan, I don't know what to think. We only have one car right now and we're not planning to get a second one till fall, so I'm pretty much tied down to the house when Craig is at work. The other morning after Craig drove off to the office I heard a noise in the garage. I went out there and saw someone I thought was Craig."

"Did he speak to you?"

"He muttered something about forgetting his briefcase and then went out again. But our car wasn't in the driveway. He simply walked down the road. I phoned his office later and he said it wasn't him. You know the rest. I insisted he hire a detective."

"Was Craig married before?"

"Yes. He was divorced five years ago."

"Any chance his first wife bears a grudge?"

"Why should she? He certainly made a generous settlement!"

"Is she here in the city?"

"No, she moved to Arizona after the divorce. There were no children." Her eyes kept shifting to Mike, and she asked him, "Don't you have any questions for me?"

He blushed and said, "Al is handling it pretty well."

As she saw us to the door she asked, "Is my husband in danger?"

"Possibly. We're checking out every angle."

We left her standing in the doorway of the fashionable ranch home and drove back to the city. "She seems quite nice," Mike commented.

"Watch yourself, kid. That kind could eat you alive."

"I just meant—"

"I know. Look, I've got a surprise for you on the way back."

"What sort of surprise?"

"You'll see."

I took him to the gun shop and produced the permit he'd signed for the police. The clerk handed over the .38 Terrier and I thought Mike's eyes would pop out of his head. "This is mine?" he asked.

"Yeah. A little gift. Do you want a shoulder or belt holster for it?"

"I don't know. What do you think?"

"A belt holster's a lot cooler in the summer."

"Sounds good to me."

"I've arranged with Sergeant O'Keefe for you to use the police pistol range for practice."

As we left the gun shop he said, "We make a pretty good team, don't we?"

"Not bad. I'll tell you better when we see what happens with the Winton case."

Later that afternoon I took him to the bar around the corner for a drink. "You ever been married, Al?" he asked me.

"Yeah, when I was a kid about your age."

"What happened?"

I shrugged. "Nothing. I guess kids today are smarter to live together. One day we just decided to call it quits."

"Have you got any family?"

"Parents are both dead. I've got a sister who sends me Christmas cards."

"Isn't it sort of lonely? Didn't you ever want to get married again?"

"Sure, kid." I gave him a smile. "Maybe I will some day."

"What about the Winton case? What should I do?"

I pulled out a copy of Craig Winton's schedule. "Cover him like we discussed. Look for anyone who resembles him and is dressed like him. Meanwhile I'll go talk to his secretary."

I did that the next day but I didn't learn much. Winton was a middle-level executive with the insurance company and she was a middle-level secretary. Her name was Milly Scorese and she was a fortyish redhead, a bit overweight. When I mentioned it, she remembered the month-old incident. "Oh, yes. Mr. Winton seemed quite disturbed by it."

"Did the man speak to you at all?"

"No. He entered through that private door and went right into Mr. Winton's office."

"So no one else saw him?"

"No."

"Did you get a good look at him?"

"Well," she admitted, "more at his clothes than at him. He went by my desk so fast I just got a glimpse of the pink sports jacket Mr. Winton was wearing that day. But I certainly thought it was him. When he left a few minutes later it looked like him from the rear. But he didn't speak."

I gave her a smile. "Thanks, Milly. Look, here's my card. If anything unusual like that happens again, call me right away."

"I'll help any way I can. Mr. Winton told me to cooperate."

On my way out of the office I thought I saw Winton ahead of me, getting on the elevator. I hurried to catch up, but it wasn't him. I decided there were a lot of tall white-haired men in the business world.

The case dragged on for a couple of weeks without noticeable progress. I saw Mike Trapper only during the hours when Winton was safely in his office with no plans to leave. The rest of the time Mike was watching the Winton home, or shadowing him at business meetings. Once, when Winton flew to New York, the kid went ahead on an earlier flight and was at the airport to pick up the trail when our client landed.

But there was no sign of the double.

"Maybe only Winton can see him," Mike speculated one evening after he'd trailed him home.

"You're back to your doppelgangers again."

"I just like to consider all the possibilities." He had a sudden thought. "Hey, my dad's in town tonight and I'm meeting him for a late dinner. Come along with us! I know he's been wanting to meet you."

"Well, it's sort of short notice," I replied.

"Come on! He'll love it!"

James Trapper was a stout friendly man who wore thick glasses and a checked vest. "I never imagined Mike would end up the partner in a detective agency," he admitted. "How's he doing, Mr. Darlan?"

"He's learning."

"Had any good murder cases yet?"

I laughed. "I haven't had a case involving murder in four years. They don't come along every week, despite what you see on TV."

Dinner was pleasant, and somehow they made me feel like part of the family. It was a good feeling. At one point James Trapper said, "Mike's always had an eye for the ladies. You've probably noticed that already."

"I've noticed they have an eye for him," I said, remembering our client's wife. "But I keep him pretty busy."

As we were leaving the restaurant Mike asked me, "How long we going to keep on with this Winton case?"

"As long as he pays us. Speaking of Winton, I have an appointment to meet with one of the vice-presidents at his insurance company tomorrow morning. I'll let you know if I learn anything. What's Winton's schedule?"

"Routine during the day, but he has a Civic Club meeting in the evening, out at the Expressway Motel."

I nodded. "I'll check with you tomorrow. It's been better than two weeks. The double might be getting ready to show himself again."

James Trapper shook my hand at the car. "It's been a pleasure, Mr. Darlan."

"Please call me Al."

"I know my son is in good hands, Al."

"I hope so."

The next morning I met with Isaac Rath in the executive suite of Winton's company. He was a balding man in his sixties, with brown spots on the backs of his hands. He frowned at me and said, "I don't quite understand the reason for this meeting, Mr. Darlan."

"Craig Winton has hired me about a personal matter. I'd be interested in anything you could tell me about him."

Isaac Rath touched the tips of his fingers together. "Craig is one of the finest executives. He runs our investments division and has full authority over a good share of company funds."

"I know that much already. I guess what I'm getting at is this. Would it be possible for someone impersonating Winton to get his hands on any large amount of company money?"

"Impersonating—? I don't understand."

I tried to make it simple. "Could Craig Winton, or someone pretending to be Craig Winton, steal any money from this company?"

"Well, of course! He could divert investments into phoney accounts. He could—"

"Thank you, Mr. Rath. That's all I wanted to know."

I went back to the office and waited for the kid to call in. I waited all afternoon and never heard from him. Finally I went home to my apartment, hoping nothing was wrong. It was after dark, around ten o'clock, when the phone finally rang.

"Al?"

"Mike! Where in hell are you?"

"At the Expressway Motel." His voice sounded awful. "Al, could you get out here fast? Craig Winton's dead. Somebody shot him in the parking lot."

"OK, kid. Are the cops there?"

"I just called them."

"I'll be along."

I had to drive through downtown anyway, so I went up to the office for just a minute. I got my revolver out of the old iron safe.

A ring of police cars had their spotlights trained on the body as I walked up. The police photographer was snapping pictures and Sergeant O'Keefe was standing off to one side. I got near enough to see that Winton had been shot at least once in the center of the chest. Then I went over to O'Keefe.

"That was your client?" he asked, looking up from his notebook. "His wife's driving down to make an official identification."

"Yeah. Where's the kid?"

"Trapper? Inside with one of my boys. His story is that he was waiting in his car for Winton to leave the meeting. Apparently Winton decided to leave early, before the meeting broke up. Trapper didn't see him, but he heard a shot. He found Winton dead between a couple of parked cars, with no one else around."

"I want to see him," I said. "Now."

O'Keefe led me into the motel. Mike was seated in a corner of the lobby with one of the detectives. He looked terrible. O'Keefe motioned his man away and let me have a few words alone with the kid.

"Look," I said, "first of all, it's not your fault. There's nothing you could have done."

He looked like he was going to cry. "I bungled it, Al. And now he's dead!"

"Tell me everything that happened, right from the beginning. When's the last time you saw him alive?"

"When he drove his car up to the motel and went inside."

"How come you didn't check in with me this afternoon?"

He looked edgy. "I was out at Winton's house for a while, seeing if his wife had any new information."

"All right," I said with a sigh. "What happened tonight?"

"I scouted the area before Winton drove up. There was no sign of a double or anything else out of whack. He parked the car and went into his meeting. I already knew it wouldn't be over till ten o'clock so I sat in the car playing the radio. Once the meeting started I didn't notice anyone else in the parking lot at all. Winton had gone in the motel's front entrance and I figured he'd come out the same way. But he came out the side door instead. The first thing I knew, I heard a shot. I got out of the car and ran over and found him lying out there between the cars."

"There was no sign of anyone else?"

He shook his head. "I called the police, and then I phoned you. I didn't know what to do."

I had an empty feeling in the pit of my stomach. "Kid," I said quietly, "let me have your gun."

"What?"

"If you didn't see Winton before he was shot, how'd you know he came out the side door?"

"I—"

"Come on, give me your gun."

He froze then, staring at me with that terrible expression on his face, and I wondered what I would do if he resisted. My fingers were only inches from my gun, but I knew I couldn't shoot him any more than I could have shot my own son.

His shoulders slumped and he pulled the revolver from its belt holster. I took it and opened the cylinder. All five chambers were loaded but I could catch the unmistakable scent of gunpowder in the barrel. It had been fired recently. "You killed him, didn't you, kid?"

He couldn't meet my eyes. "Yeah," he said huskily, close to tears. "I killed him."

I put my hand on his shoulder. "Was it that wife of his, Mike?"

He raised his head then. "Is that what you think? She had nothing to do with it! I was watching for the double and Winton came out the wrong door, a half hour early. I called to him and he acted funny, started going the other way. When I went after him he pulled out something that looked like a gun. I panicked and shot him."

"Why didn't you tell the police that?"

"Because I was scared when I saw that I'd killed the real Winton. The police didn't find any weapon by the body and I knew I'd made a terrible mistake. Don't you realize that?"

I realized it. I realized I'd have to phone his dad and tell him what had happened. He'd been too fast to pull a trigger, and we were both going to pay for it.

I walked over and handed the gun to O'Keefe.

"Here's your murder weapon," I said. "The kid's ready to tell the truth now. For God's sake, go easy on him."

I didn't go home that night. Instead I went back to the office and sat in my swivel chair staring out at the city. I wanted to go down to Headquarters just to be near him, but I knew there was nothing I could do for him now. After a long time I fell asleep in my chair, and when I woke up it was morning.

I drove through the streets only beginning to come awake, not knowing at first just where I was headed. I passed out of downtown, away from the jail where they'd be holding Mike until his dad came up with the bail money. I just drove.

After a while it came to me where I was headed. Maybe I'd known all along. The suburban traffic was all headed into the city as the morning rush hour began, and I made good time going against the stream. It was just eight o'clock when I pulled into the driveway of the Winton ranch home. Craig Winton's car was in the garage.

It took me five minutes of ringing the doorbell before she'd answer. When she finally came she was wearing a rumpled T-shirt and faded jeans, looking like she was dead instead of her husband.

"God, what is it? What do you want? Haven't you done enough to us already?"

"I'd like to come in, Mrs. Winton. It's very important."

She seemed ready to bar my way, but finally she stepped aside. "You'll have to forgive me," she said, passing a hand over her eyes. "I took a sleeping pill and I just woke up."

"I'm sorry about what happened to your husband."

"Is it true that Mike Trapper killed him?"

"I'm afraid so."

"He was just here yesterday asking more questions. He was really trying to help us. How could he have killed Craig?"

"I drove out here to ask the same question." I'd followed her into the kitchen and taken a chair across the table from her.

"Do you want some coffee?"

"That would be fine." She rose to make it and I continued, "Your husband's death still leaves the problem of the double unresolved."

"It hardly matters now. Just send me your bill."

"It's not as simple as that."

"Why not?"

"There wasn't any double, was there, Mrs. Winton? It was Craig Winton all the time."

She turned from the coffee percolator. "I don't know what you're talking about."

"It was a scheme of Craig's to embezzle money from his company, and a clever scheme at that. He created a double who made a few appearances. He even hired a two-bit private detective agency to find the double. Last night was to be a key element of his plan. Mike Trapper would testify to having seen the double. He'd know it wasn't our client because the double would run from him and even draw a gun. Unfortunately for Craig Winton, he didn't know that a nervous kid like Mike, investigating his first case, would shoot and kill him."

"That's guesswork." She poured two cups of coffee.

"Not entirely," I said. "Craig's secretary, Milly, told me the double didn't speak to her. At first this made sense but then I remembered the supposed double had spoken to you in the garage here. If his voice could fool you it could certainly fool his secretary. Yet he hurried in and out of the office, giving Milly only a glimpse. It didn't sound like a true impersonation to me. It sounded like someone trying to fake an impersonation. The same goes for the two earlier events. Craig made a fuss at the hotel and at the meeting just so the incidents would be remembered."

"It still could have been a double."

"Then consider this. That day at the office Milly saw the supposed double wearing a pink sports jacket like Craig's. And obviously he was wearing the same clothes as Craig that day in the garage. Duplicating those clothes—the correct clothes for each day—would be next to impossible, unless you believe in the supernatural. Either the double had prior knowledge of each day's costume, or there was no double. Either way Craig had to be involved in the plot."

"I don't know a thing about that," she insisted.

"I believe you do, Mrs. Winton. You were there last night when Mike shot your husband in the parking lot."

"What? That's insane!"

"Is it? The first time I spoke to you I learned the two of you had only one car, and didn't plan to buy another one till fall. Mike saw Winton drive up to the motel in that car last night, yet the police made no mention of the car later. O'Keefe even told me you were driving over to identify the body. And the car is sitting in your garage right now. How did it get from the motel parking lot back to this house before the police called, unless you were there to drive it back?"

"I—"

"Mike said he saw a gun in Winton's hand, yet by the time the police arrived there was no sign of one. That's one reason the kid tried to lie about the shooting. I think you saw it all from nearby. When Mike ran into the motel to phone the police and me, you hurried over to the body, picked up the gun, and drove the car home. You didn't want the police finding the gun and guessing this double business had been part of an embezzlement scheme. And you had to take the car because you couldn't risk a cab driver identifying you later. And you had to be home before the police called."

"All right," she said quietly. The fight had gone out of her.

"You admit you took the gun?"

"It was only a starter's pistol. Craig wasn't going to harm anyone. He simply wanted your partner's testimony that a double existed. He'd been manipulating his company's money for years, ever since that big divorce settlement took all his cash. He tried to create a double who could be blamed for unauthorized bank withdrawals and other shady business. It was a far-fetched scheme, but it would have been enough to raise a reasonable doubt in any jury's mind."

"What about the car?"

"I took a cab to the motel hours earlier for just that purpose. After Mike saw him Craig planned to jump in a cab and get away. While Mike was chasing him I was to drive the car home, as if Craig had come out of his meeting and left with it. When Mike returned to the lot and found Craig's car gone, it would be extra proof there must be two Craig Wintons."

I finished my coffee. "Mike's in jail and you're the only one who can get him out. I want you to come with me and tell all this to the police."

"Is he that important to you?"

"I guess he is. I want him out."

Our eyes met for just an instant. She may have been trying to tell me something, to offer me something, but we both knew it was useless.

She picked up her purse and I followed her out to the car.

The Scoop

JOSEPH L. KOENIG

For the past fifteen years Joseph Koenig has written true crime articles for pulp magazines. "The Scoop" is his first published fiction, except for what he describes as "a couple of very short pieces for a pulp that went belly-up."

There are two sources for "The Scoop." The plot is based on a true story that circulated some years ago involving the female editor of a true crime magazine. The technique was inspired by Ring Lardner's "Haircut."

Mr. Koenig's first novel will be published this year.

SO THIS IS the new fella. You're only an hour late's what gives it away. Solly mentioned he was sending you up. Must be he still has a soft spot for the Lincoln County bureau, 'cause we get all the eager beavers. Just lift your feet and let me sweep underneath a bit. The newsies don't usually start dropping by till happy hour's done.

Bet you didn't know Solly won his stripes here. Before he got his legs broke he was a real eager beaver himself. If he wasn't waking the DA for a perp's middle initial, he'd be snatching some stiff's picture right off the crate to run in the obits. Else you'd find him down to the sheriff's office collecting the john list from Maybry's vice dicks. Judge Walker okayed seventeen divorces the year he done that and in a county the size of Lincoln it's some kind of record. Lot of folks'd shot him if they got the chance, but Solly passed the blame like shit through a goose. Said it's a reporter's job to print all the facts and let the chips fall where they may. Solly's one fella still has principles.

He put in for cityside during the big to-do what followed and just like that he's the *Tattler*'s state editor. So far as I know, he's only been back once, for the Rheinhold murder case. It was a regular tragedy, that was. Nutty Henry Rheinhold, one night when the folks was asleep he hacked 'em all to shreds, his pa, the missus, his granddad, Becky, and Steve, even the cat. Covered up what he done by torching the place and damned if he didn't lose the barn and the henhouse too.

The funny thing is Henry was maybe the sanest one of all them Rheinholds. Half the time you'd swear the boy was better'n normal. During the Optimists' picnic Judge Walker's granddaughter fell in the Clear River directly above the dam and Henry was the only fella there with presence of mind to jump in and paddle the little tyke back to shore. Walker was so grateful he offered Henry money, a car, anything, you name it. All Henry wanted was a golf ball, so he could crack it open on a rock and play with the liquid center inside.

Anyways, after the big fire at the Rheinholds, Maybry counted up the bodies, and when he seen Henry's wasn't none of 'em it didn't take a genius to figure out what must've happened. He scouted around till he found the boy camped out in the sugar bush back of where the barn used to be. Buck naked and baying at the moon, Maybry said. He wrapped him in a blanket and brung him in and booked him for murder, five counts' worth. Judge Walker got on the horn to the state institution and warned the docs he'd be sending over a live one soon as the legal formalities was out of the way. Keeping him out of the penitentiary was the least he could do, after all.

The Lincoln County bureau was a one-man show back then, and when Pris Johnson, the new gal, heard they'd been an arrest, she couldn't get to the jailhouse quick enough to see what's in it for her. Maybry lived in fear of the *Tattler,* so he give her the run of the place, and Pris had a field day with Henry. The crazy dished out all the poop on how the cherubs and archangels was asking to see the folks and that's why he'd sent them on up ahead, and then he wanted to know what that old Speed Graphic of Pris's was for. Pris showed him all right. She went down low with her flash and shot straight up on him, so's his puss caught the light like he was the devil incarnate. Solly hung the pix over the masthead and circulation topped out for weeks.

When Judge Walker got a look at the *Tattler*, he like to throw a fit. Had Pris Johnson hauled into court and told her she'd good as got Henry killed. What with all the ink, there's no way he could sneak the boy off to the laughing academy, where he belonged. The DA'd jump-start the chair before he picked a jury. Pris shrugged and said she was sorry, but she was just doing her job. Walker done the same and give her thirty days for contempt.

Now, it's no big secret how Solly'd made state editor, and it wasn't his sunny disposition or that pug-ugly kisser he's wearing today that done it. What he had going for him was even features and Sue McDonough, the publisher's old lady, who he was doing weekends and holiday nights on the foreign desk. Sue was real upset over what happened to Pris. Solly told her not to worry; no hick judge was going to clap one of his top legmen in the slammer.

Soon's he put the Friday P.M. edition to bed, Solly hustled himself up to Lincoln. He moved pretty good before his hips was busted, and by suppertime he was banging on Judge Walker's door saying, "We gotta talk."

His Honor'd been looking forward to chatting with Solly, so his answer is, "You bet. Only thing," he says, "I wasn't expecting company, let's do it at the courthouse." When Solly comes in his chambers, Walker's got on his robes and he ain't interested in a lecture about the First Amendment. All he knows is Pris Johnson has just about got Henry Rheinhold legally lynched by the state and someone's gotta pay.

"I could care less," Solly tells him right off. "This ain't Russia; they got freedom of the press in this country in case you ain't heard. Gimme back my reporter."

Walker turns up his hearing aid 'cause he don't believe he's getting this straight. Only he is, of course, and while Solly's still warming up Walker tells him he's holding him in contempt of court, just like Pris. Solly's trying to top that one when Maybry brings him down to the lockup and takes away his Swiss army knife and his shoelaces.

Solly's pinching hard to a dime, but Maybry tells him it's too late to make bond so forget about trying and ain't it a shame he has to spend the whole weekend in jail, is there anything he'd like besides a cake with a file for the filling. It suddenly hits Solly where he's stuck at, and he's feeling so low he just dives on the cot and shuts his eyes. And he don't open 'em again till he feels a poke in his ribs.

Solly thinks it's the *Tattler*'s lawyer come to spring him, but when he rolls over he's looking at the most wild-eyed creature he's ever had the misfortune to see. It's a fella, he finally decides, and sort of familiar looking at that, but it's hard to say who 'cause his face is streaked with dirt, and his cheeks are running with blood where he's dug them open with fingernails like daggers, and his hair is matted down over his eyes. Top of everything else, he's babbling in a whole bunch of tongues, none of which Solly is acquainted with.

Seeing as how they're bunking together, Solly figures it ain't a bad idea to make friends. "What's a nice fella like you doin' in a place like this?" he tries for openers.

"What'm I doing here? I'm out of my mind, can't you see?" To prove it he cracks his head against the bars so hard Solly's begins to throb. "I'm nuts, and if Maybry'd notice he'd take me out of this miserable dungeon and put me in a nice clean hospital where I can play knock rummy and watch 'General Hospital' to my heart's content."

"Is that all?" Solly says. "Well then, what's the problem?"

"The problem's that I brung my folks to their heavenly reward and now the goddamn *Tattler*'s on my case and I can't get justice nohow. They're fixing to give me the hot squat. But I'm cuckoo, ain't I? If I can only find a way to show 'em."

Then he cools off just like that and hunkers down on the cot and wraps a paw around Solly's shoulders. Solly don't care for the smell, but he don't push him away either 'cause Henry Rheinhold, I forgot to mention, is one very large boy. And then Henry says in a voice as smooth as a shrink's, "But enough about my troubles. . . . What brings you here?"

You can put your feet down now.

There's No Such Thing as Private Eyes

MARK COGGINS

Mark Coggins is a computer programmer who studied international relations at Stanford and hopes to be a full-time professional writer. "There's No Such Thing as Private Eyes" is his first published story, and he plans to expand it into a novel. He is twenty-seven.

DELBERT EVANS was cheap: cheap with his time, cheap with his money. Cheap with everything. It didn't do you any good to tell him, though, because he liked being that way. I was sitting at a table of the cheap bar we had agreed upon when he came up—thirty minutes late.

Delbert sold insurance. I don't know how, but he did. I guess people bought it because they felt sorry for Delbert when they got their first look at him. His head was wedge-shaped, almost all profiles. His nose was a full-scale copy of Edison's first light bulb, and his eyes were close set and slightly crossed. The rest of him wasn't much better. He had a stick body that his Sears suits never fit and feet so long a cow gave up its life every time he went to buy shoes. Delbert made a nervous gesture I took for a wave, bumped the table sitting down, and said:

"Excuse me for being late, August. I got caught on the phone with a very important call, and I didn't leave my office until just a few minutes ago."

I laughed like I didn't believe him. "Okay, Del, why did you call me down here?"

Delbert smiled and capped teeth shone behind his thick lips. "You private investigators are always in a hurry," he complained. "Couldn't you allow me to order a drink before we get down to business?"

I said that I could.

Delbert signaled a waitress and ordered one of those sweet, candied drinks people are always inventing nowadays. I asked for another Scotch.

"Here's the proposition," Delbert said after the waitress had gone. "We want you to investigate the theft of an expensive diamond pendant that was insured by our company. We are prepared to offer you 10 percent of its insured value if you recover it. Otherwise, we will pay you at the rate of $100 a day plus expenses for the time you spend on the investigation."

That was unusual. Insurance companies rarely offered to pay a daily rate for recovery investigations. I said, "What's the catch, Del? I know you guys don't work that way."

Delbert's face became flushed. "Yes, well, the pendant is worth over $500,000, so naturally the insurance company is very concerned about recovering it for our client. We are offering you the rate of $100 a day even if you don't recover the pendant to insure that you will be motivated."

I still wasn't buying. Delbert was too cheap to offer more money than he had to. I rode him some with my stare.

"Ahem, of course," Delbert sputtered on, "if it should turn out that the pendant has not been stolen at all, that our client still has it, then you could not really claim to have recovered it."

"And I wouldn't be entitled to the 10 percent fee, right? I get it now. You guys think your client has faked the robbery to get hold of the insurance money and still keep the pendant. But it's cheaper to hire me at $100 a day to prove it than to pay me fifty grand."

"Ah, yes, something like that," said Delbert. "Will you take the case?"

Normally I didn't like insurance jobs, but my bank balance was so low it would fit under a lizard. I said, "Okay, make it 125 and give me the details."

Delbert smiled with relief. "$125 it is, August. Our client's name is Pamela Dyer. She is the widow of a wealthy real estate developer. The pendant was stolen a week ago from the apartment of a friend of hers, Robert Grey. Mrs. Dyer and Grey had gone to the apartment after eating dinner in a restaurant. Shortly after they arrived, two men with guns burst through the door and demanded they turn over all the valuables on their person. The men had stockings over their faces. Grey lost a gold watch and a hundred dollars in cash; Mrs. Dyer lost two diamond rings and the pendant. The gunmen tied up Mrs. Dyer and Grey before they left and pulled out the phone for good measure: Grey said he managed to free himself after an hour of struggling, and then he released Mrs. Dyer and went to a neighbor's apartment to phone the police."

The waitress came up with our drinks and scurried off. I took a few sips from mine before I said anything. Finally: "I can see why you would think the robbery was a fake, Del. The gunmen knowing Mrs. Dyer would be in Grey's apartment with the pendant at that particular time does seem unlikely. But they could have spotted the pendant in the restaurant and then followed Grey and Dyer home to make the heist."

Delbert looked disappointed. "Do you really think so?" he asked.

"No, I'm not sure. I just wanted to show you that there were two ways of looking at it. Do you know what the police think about the robbery?"

"They seem altogether satisfied that Mrs. Dyer and Grey are telling the truth. However, they don't seem to be doing much in the way of investigation. That's why we are hiring you."

I nodded in sympathetic agreement and pumped Delbert for a few more details, like the addresses of Robert Grey and Mrs. Dyer. We finished our drinks then, and I left Delbert in the bar to do whatever it is insurance salesmen do by themselves in bars.

This was Phoenix in the summertime and it was hot. I drove in my Ford Galaxy with all four windows down because the air conditioner had given out two summers ago. I was heading up Central Avenue from the bar downtown to see Pamela Dyer's boyfriend, Robert Grey. Grey was a big-wheel lawyer in Phoenix, and the firm he worked for had its offices in the posh Weckler Building on Highland.

When I came to Highland, I turned left off Central and drove a block or so until I reached the underground garage that served the cluster of office buildings in the vicinity. I parked in a cramped space on the third level, rode the elevator back upstairs, and crossed the street to the Weckler Building.

The Ringling Brothers could have fit their circus in the lobby, elephants and all. Right then it was populated by flashy, overweight business types who still wore their three-piece suits, even though it was 105 degrees outside. I walked to the elevators, losing sight of my feet a number of times in the pasture of wool they used for carpet. At the directory, I checked the number of Grey's office, and then I caught a ride on an ascending elevator to the fifth floor.

Grey's office was a short way down the hall on the right. Inside I found a cute secretary making noise with an electric typewriter. She had long blond hair and a deeply tanned oval face. She wore a cream pantsuit over a figure that would make an accountant snap his pencils. I introduced myself by giving her one of the smudged business cards I carried around in my wallet and asked if I might see Mr. Grey about the theft of Mrs. Dyer's pendant. She walked distractingly back to a dark-grained wooden door, knocked lightly, went in.

When she returned, I was told Mr. Grey would allow me ten minutes of his time. Grey was a fat man, but it didn't seem to bother him. He waltzed around his desk to greet me like someone who weighed seventy pounds less. The grip he clamped on my hand was very firm. The light brown hair on his head was beginning to thin out, and he had a pleasant face that would have been handsome except for his extra chins. He wore a lightweight navy blue suit.

After we exchanged pleasantries and sat down, I said, "Mr. Grey, I've been hired by the insurance company to investigate the theft of Mrs. Dyer's pendant, and I was wondering if you could give me some information about it."

Grey smiled faintly and formed a bridge with his hands. "You must realize that I have already given all the information I know about the theft to the police, Mr. Hammond. There is no need for anyone to question me further. I think the insurance company is stalling, and you are merely part of that stall. How much longer will Pamela have to wait before they give her the money she is entitled to?"

"Ask them. They think you two faked the robbery," I said just to rattle him.

Grey looked about as rattled as a granite headstone.

He frowned and pushed his real chin down into the other ones. "You can't be serious. Mrs. Dyer and I were robbed and tied up in my apartment by two very real thugs. There was no duplicity involved."

"What did the men look like?"

"They wore stockings over their faces."

"So I've been told. But can you describe the rest of them?"

"They were both moderately tall with strong builds. And they both wore Levi's and T-shirts. I can't tell you anything more."

"Okay," I said. "Did you notice anyone like them following you from the restaurant after dinner?"

"No, I did not. Of course, I wasn't really looking."

"How often did Mrs. Dyer wear her pendant?"

Grey let out a big long sigh like he was tired of talking about the whole thing. "She wore it occasionally," he said. "She did not wear it all the time like some women do with expensive jewelry. Pamela has very good taste."

"Yeah, in some things."

Grey's face reddened. "What is that supposed to mean, Hammond?"

"I forgot. When was the—"

Grey cut me off. He said, "I don't care to discuss this any further. If you want more information, then go ask the police. Perhaps they have time to waste with cretins."

"Lots. They talked to you, didn't they?"

I was a real friendly guy that afternoon. I got up and went through the door. Grey's secretary was still typing in the outer office. She looked up from her work and addressed me in a cheery tone:

"Did you get what you came for?"

"Yeah," I said. "I got what I came for. But now that I'm here, I see something else I might like too." I smiled a cute smile and waited for her to catch on. I didn't wait much.

"You can't always get what you want. Bye-bye, Mr. Hammond."

I laughed a little, winked at her, went out the door.

My office would never win any awards for interior decoration, or anything else for that matter. I leased it in a building that used to be a profitable hotel until the neighborhood ran down and they turned it into an office building for seedy businessmen like myself. There were a few seedy dentists in the building too. Anyway, my office still looked like a hotel room with a small bedroom off the hallway door and an even smaller bathroom adjoining it. I'd filled the bedroom with a secondhand sofa that was also a foldaway bed, an elementary school teacher's desk I'd bought at a sale when the school burned down, a filing cabinet I got from the same school, and two chairs: one for myself and one for my client. The bathroom I'd filled with a lot of air.

I was lying flat out on the sofa, holding a glass of whiskey on the middle of my stomach. I had eaten dinner in my apartment and come back here to think. The most conclusive decision I'd come to since lying there was that the ceiling was dirty. The second most conclusive decision I'd reached was that I should call Pamela Dyer. I moved to the desk to carry it out.

I rang her number a long time before the maid answered. I identified myself and asked to speak to Mrs. Dyer. A few seconds later, she came on.

"Hello, Mr. Hammond. Robert said that you might try to contact me. I don't believe I have anything to say to you, though." Her voice was hard and distant.

"Don't you want to recover your pendant?"

"Yes, of course. But I've been answering questions for a week now, and still I don't have it back. Answering questions doesn't seem to do any good, Mr. Hammond."

"Let's try some of mine anyway. Can you describe the pendant for me?"

There was a short pause. "Oh very well," she said. "The pendant is made of gold and is shaped like a heart, or the outline of a heart. It's strung on a fine chain, which is also made of gold. There are blue diamonds inlaid along the circumference. The diamond at the top cusp is larger than the others and is of unusually fine quality. That diamond is what makes the pendant so valuable: it's one of the largest blue diamonds in the world."

"Oh," I said. It sounded pretty gaudy to me. Maybe Mrs. Dyer didn't have good taste in anything. "How did you acquire the pendant?"

"My late husband gave it to me for our tenth anniversary."

"How long ago was that?"

"None of your business," she snapped.
"Right; but how long ago was it?"

She made a snarling sound. I hardly recognized her voice as she barked, "Go fry your face in a pan, Hammond." Then she hung up.

My mouth fell open like it usually does. Nothing in there but teeth and stale air. I was really pumping 'em dry. No scrap of information escaped detective Hammond. He knows all the right questions and all the right ways to ask them.

I wheeled back in my chair to the filing cabinet and opened the drawer with the only thing important in it to get a bottle of whiskey. I poured an inch or so of the stuff into my glass. It wasn't very good, but I took my medicine and liked it. I was going to see Mrs. Dyer in person, and I needed all the help I could get.

She lived in a ritzy section of north Phoenix. I didn't have any trouble locating the house because it was as big as a barn—and only a bit more handsome. It was lit up like some kind of government building with floodlights that shone up from the ground. I pulled into the circle drive and parked my dusty Ford behind a shiny new Mercedes. At least my car was in good company; I knew I wouldn't be with Pamela Dyer.

I crossed to the front door and banged on it with the ornate knocker that hung there. After a while the porch light came on, and a tall woman in a black crepe dress answered the door. She was forty or so, big-boned and rugged looking. Her hair, black as her dress, was wound tightly in a severe bun many years out of style.

She looked me over slowly with an expression most people save for child molesters and Bolsheviks. It had to be Pamela Dyer.

"Who are you?" she asked sternly.

"Hammond," I said. "August Hammond."

"You're the private investigator who called, then?"

"Yeah."

Her eyes burned greenly. "Come in," she said, and led me into a large sunken living room.

I looked around. The room was a fine illustration of what a lot of money and no taste can accomplish. Antique furniture from twelve different periods cluttered it. Expensive-looking pictures hung on all four walls at irregular intervals, and a large Persian rug lay in the middle of the floor on top of the regular carpet.

There was also a tall man with a big gun in the far right corner.

I said, "Is that your maid, Mrs. Dyer?"

The man began laughing like a sick horse and walked in to the middle of the room, pointing his Colt Army .45 at me. "That's right, smart guy," he said. "I'm the maid and I'm here to do a little housecleaning. Check him for a gun, Pammie."

There wasn't anywhere to check except my belt line because I didn't have a jacket on, just short sleeves. I don't carry a gun unless I think I'll need it, and I didn't think that night. Mrs. Dyer patted my waistline anyway—about as firmly as you'd caress a hot stove. She stepped back when she was finished, and the tall guy with the gun came up and dug it into my stomach.

His big red face was pitted with acne scars, and his breath smelled of liquor. But so did mine.

He said, "Pammie doesn't like smart-guy private detectives tracking their gumshoe prints all over her neat little house, so she called me to help her clean up. What do you think of that, smart guy?"

"It's fine—if she wants to fumigate after you leave."

He didn't like that one, and he told me so by swinging the flat of the .45 into my left cheek—hard. I staggered back but didn't fall. I got mad then and decided to take my chances. Pockface had the gun pointed to the side because of the follow-through on his swing. I lunged toward his gun arm, bringing my knee up into his groin as I came forward. A half second later, we both hit the ground and he lost his grip on the .45. I slugged him once in the jaw and struggled across the Persian rug to reach the gun. I would have made it too, if Pamela Dyer hadn't hit me in the back of the head with one of her antique chairs.

My arms buckled under me then, and I began to lose consciousness. The last thing I remembered was Pockface kicking me in the ribs. It's funny, but I hardly felt it at all.

The sun peeped through a crack in some expensive curtains, and a wonderful day began outside. I felt like throwing up.

I was lying face down on the Persian rug in Mrs. Dyer's sunken living room. Beside me lay the remains of what had once been an Italian antique chair. Or maybe it was French; I'm not an expert. I knew without checking that the back of my head was missing. I checked anyway and found a matted patch of bloody hair on a bump big enough to convince me that my head was reproducing by fission.

As for my ribs, I decided it would be less painful if I just stopped breathing.

The sun had moved several degrees higher in the sky before I forced myself to consider getting up. I glanced at my watch; it was 7:30. If I didn't get up soon, the real maid would come along and vacuum me off the rug. I struggled to my feet and surveyed the room from an upright position. There was no one in it.

I checked the rest of the rooms and didn't find anyone else. None of the beds had been slept in. I went into the kitchen and put some ice in a baggie for the back of my head. I found the front door then and walked to my car.

The sun was so bright outside that for a full five minutes I couldn't do anything but stand by my car squinting, holding the ice to the back of my head. As I stood there, I heard the morning traffic on a main street about a quarter mile away. Slowly, my eyes adjusted to the stark light, and I could see normally again. I did not like what I saw. Pamela Dyer lay hunched up in the backseat of my car looking dead.

I jerked the door open and felt for a pulse. There wasn't any. Her black hair had fallen from the tight bun and settled around her shoulders in coarse, tangled strands. It gave her a frivolous kind of appearance I wouldn't have thought possible. Her neck above the crepe dress was blotched with dark bruises: she had been strangled. The body was stiff and cold, growing stiffer and colder. I went around to the trunk of the car and got out an old blanket I kept there. I wrapped her carefully in the blanket, placed the body inside the trunk, closed it. My ribs were smarting the whole time.

I eased myself into the car and pulled out of the driveway. As I left, I noticed the Mercedes from last night was missing. I didn't know where I was going; I was just getting away from there.

I ended up at a small city park at the northern edge of Phoenix. I drove up to one of the covered picnic tables they call ramadas and parked the car. When I was sure no one was around, I opened the trunk and hefted Pamela Dyer's body onto the picnic table. It was a gruesome job.

I got in my car again and aimed it toward an open coffee shop. I went first to the bathroom to wash my face. There was a large bruise on my left cheek, and the skin was broken. I had almost forgotten about it with all the other rough stuff that had happened to me. I bent my head over the sink and tried to wash out some of the dried blood that was caked in my hair. I patted my hair dry with a paper towel, then went out to get some breakfast.

The waitress thought I'd been run over by a truck, and she told me so. I ordered a lot—not because I was hungry, but because I needed food—and began scanning a morning paper someone had left behind. I half expected to see a headline reading, "Private Investigator Strangles Woman and Hides Body in Park." It wasn't there, however.

The food came and I ate it. It didn't taste very good, but I felt less light-headed with something in my stomach. After I finished, I went back to a pay phone and dialed the police department to tell them they would find the body of a dead woman at the park. It would take them several days to identify the body, especially if the media didn't pick up on it. I needed those days to figure out the mess and clear myself against the time someone finally reported Mrs. Dyer missing.

I got into the car one last time and drove to Delbert Evans's office. I had to talk to someone.

When I got to Delbert's office, no one was there but Delbert. It was 8:50. I found him rummaging around the secretary's desk looking for a paper clip. He greeted me with a grimace and told me I looked like I had been run over by a truck. I guess waitresses and insurance salesmen think the same.

We went into the inner office and sat down. Delbert put on a brave, expectant face and said, "Well, August, how is the investigation going?"

"Mrs. Dyer is dead."

Delbert jerked like he had been shocked digging his bread out of the toaster with a fork. His face turned two shades whiter. "How did it happen?" he asked breathlessly.

I told him the whole wad, starting with my visit to

Grey's office and ending with the disposal of Mrs. Dyer's body. He sank lower and lower in his chair as I told the story, and by the time I was finished, his chest was at the same level as the desk top. "August," he said, and pulled himself up. "We hired you to find the pendant, not to antagonize Mr. Grey and Mrs. Dyer, and certainly not to have Mrs. Dyer killed."

That wasn't quite straight, but I let it slide.

"And frankly," Delbert continued, "I don't think it was very wise of you to remove Mrs. Dyer's body from the premises. You've just made it that much more difficult for the police to solve the murder and clear you."

"Be serious, Del. If I had called the police from the house when I found the body, clearing me would have been the last thing on their minds. I would be their number-one suspect. As it stands now, I'll still be the guy they go after when they identify the body. The maid who works at the house knows I talked to Mrs. Dyer last night because she answered the phone. She might even have been at the house when I got conked; I don't know."

"But what about the man with the gun? Wouldn't the police suspect him?"

"They would if they'd believe what I told 'em. But cops would as soon listen to winos in the street as private investigators."

"What are you going to do then, August?"

"Go on with the investigation. Mrs. Dyer's death and the theft of the pendant must be related. I don't know exactly where the gunboy at the house fits in, but he's got to be the link between the two. It's clear Mrs. Dyer wasn't telling us the whole story."

Delbert started to ramble on the way he did whenever he got excited. Chiefly, he was concerned that I be more careful and not involve myself or the insurance company in any more murders. I couldn't argue with that. I tried to calm him down anyway, and I spent another fifteen minutes or so talking with him about his golf game. I wouldn't know a five iron if you hit me over the head with it, but I faked it.

I left after scrounging the first name of Mrs. Dyer's maid from Delbert—that was all he knew—and went home to my apartment. There I licked my wounds and helped recycle aluminum by drinking a few beers.

The name Evita and a ten-dollar bribe were all the clerk at Valley Domestic Service needed to supply me with the full name and address of Mrs. Dyer's maid. Her full name was Evita Salaiz, and she lived on East Roosevelt in a very bad neighborhood. In fact, she lived about three blocks south of my office.

The house was a gray stucco number built around 1803. The lawn surrounding it had been planted in the same year but wasn't around now to tell the tale. Two yellowish bed sheets hung from a rusty clothesline in the side yard, providing the only shade for the whole place. A maroon Packard stood decaying nearby. I went up a cracked sidewalk to the porch and knocked at the screen door.

The Roman Empire rose and fell in the time it took someone to answer the door. The someone was a dark woman in a short white slip and nylon panty hose. Her breasts were round and obscenely full, her thighs big and muscular. She smiled at me and tilted her hips at an insolent angle. She looked about as hard to get as the time of day.

"Miss Evita Salaiz?" I asked.

"Yes," she said huskily, "that's me."

"May I come in? I'd like to talk to you about one of the people you work for."

"No, you cannot come in," she said, and effectively blocked my way with her chest. "Who are you?"

I tried to look past her into the house, but the room was too dark. "My name is August Hammond," I said in something like an official tone. "I'm the insurance investigator assigned to Mrs. Dyer's case. Did you work at her home yesterday?"

"Yes, I work for Mrs. Dyer Mondays, Wednesdays, and Fridays . . . Hey, wait a minute, you're the private detective that called yesterday evening, aren't you. I heard Mrs. Dyer talking to you on the phone, and she was not pleased. I shouldn't be talking to you." She moved to go back inside.

"Just a second," I said, and grabbed her bare arm. "I just have a few questions to ask and I don't think they'll be that painful to answer." I pulled another ten dollars from my pocket.

She thought about the money for a second. "Okay," she said. "What is it you want to know?"

"When did you leave Mrs. Dyer's house last night?"

"I left after cleaning the mess from dinner. Mrs. Dyer always has me clean up after dinner."

"Did Mrs. Dyer have any visitors yesterday?"

"No . . . no visitors."

"Are you sure?"

"Yes I'm sure. I answer the door myself when she has visitors."

"Have you ever seen a tall, red-faced man at the house?"

Someone moved in the dark room behind her. "No," she said. "I've never seen a short, blue-faced one either. Can I have my money now? I've got things to do."

I handed her the money just as a bumping noise sounded in the room. She glanced quickly behind her, pivoted, and went through the door. She locked it after her. There was nothing else to do but go back to my car and pull down the block to wait. At the least, I could tail anyone who left.

The flask from my glove box was half empty by the time her scream rang out. I hesitated only an instant before running up the street like an idiot. The house door was still locked, but the lock was cheap and it didn't last long. I pushed through to the front room and nearly tripped over her where she lay face down by the door. She looked as healthy as I'd left her—until I turned her over. The face I saw then was not the face I remembered. Her forehead was caved in like a squashed melon, thick blood and gray mash oozing from the wound. I moved to feel her pulse, doubting she had one.

I should have been smarter. I should have realized the someone I saw moving in the dark room before would still be around after he crushed her skull. I should have known. A vague figure on the edge of my vision moved toward me. It swung, brought down something hard between my shoulder blades. A painful buzzing like a swarm of bees shot up my neck and nestled in my brain. I never quite lost consciousness, but I might as well have. Darkness and the floor beneath me were all I knew.

The next minutes were long ones. I heard a lot of noises, but I couldn't distinguish any of them until I heard the sirens. The sirens were what forced me to move. Someone, probably the person who'd hit me, had called the police. I pried myself from the floor, finding Evita Salaiz's legs under me. Nearby was my candidate for the weapon that had clubbed us both: a rolling pin. It was sticky with flour and gelled blood. The front door seemed like a dumb move, so I fumbled to my feet and made for the back door. I passed through the kitchen on my way and noticed a mound of dough waiting to be rolled out. It never was.

The back door opened to an alley that ran behind the houses on my side of the block. I crept along as stealthily as my new injury would allow until I came to a gap in the alley close to my car. I walked over casually and drove. I drove past the screeching police cars stopping in front of Evita Salaiz's house and kept on driving straight to the Weckler Building. I was tired of getting beat up, and I was tired of falling over dead bodies wherever I went. I decided it was time to see Robert Grey again and really put the heat on for some useful answers.

I stuck my head through the office door and caught sight of his secretary. She was still at the desk typing, as if she had spent the whole night there. Today she was wearing a pastel summer dress.

I said, "Hi, angel, remember me?"

"Sure," she said. "How could I forget a handsome hunk like you? But, ouch, what happened to your cheek?"

I stepped inside. "One of my playmates from last night got a little rough. I'll survive."

"You always would. But I'd hate to meet any of your playmates."

"I don't see why. Any friend of mine is a friend of yours."

She flipped her hair back casually and gave me a big smile. "I already have enough friends, thank you."

"You always would. Do you think I could get in to see your employer?"

"I'll see what I can do."

Some minutes later, I found myself in Robert Grey's private office, sitting in the same chair as yesterday. Grey hadn't lost any weight in twenty-four hours, but he had changed clothes. He wore a beige suit.

"What can I do for you today, Mr. Hammond?" he asked coolly. "Have you come to exchange insults again?"

"No, but I'm still surprised you agreed to see me."

"I wouldn't have, but it seems it is the only way to

motivate the insurance company to pay Pamela's claim."

I got mean. "You needn't worry about that anymore. Mrs. Dyer is dead."

"That's preposterous."

"No, it's quite true," I said with false calm. "She was strangled to death by someone with large hands—large hands like yours maybe."

Grey looked down at his hands on the desk and then jerked them into his lap. His face reddened. "What is this, young man? Some kind of macabre joke?"

"Yeah, I'm joking. I'm also joking when I tell you Dyer's maid got her face smashed by a rolling pin. It's all something I made up. And don't call me young, because I'm not."

Grey narrowed his eyes to slits and gave me what he thought was a serious-looking stare. "Look, Hammond," he said, "I'm tired of playing this idiotic game with you. You've come into my office twice in two days, and each time you have accused me of some crime. Yesterday it was insurance fraud; today it is murder. I don't like being treated in this manner, especially by seedy private investigators. Why don't you leave before I am forced to throw you out?"

I leaned over the desk and laughed in his face. "All right, Grey, I'll leave if you don't like it. But I hope you learn how to deal with things you don't like soon. Because when I figure out this case—and believe me, I will—you are gonna like it a lot less."

Grey clamped his jaw shut and the muscles on the

side of his fleshy face twitched. I got up out of the chair and went through the door into the outer office. It had been a short meeting. The secretary wasn't in her office, so I walked straight out the next door and down the hall to the elevators. The hand I pressed the elevator button with was shaking.

I waited a time for a car to stop on the floor, and then all three showed up at once. I got into the closest one with an old guy dressed in a suit fifteen years out of style. During the ride to the lobby, he generously revealed his secret for making a million dollars. I thanked him in a tongue-in-cheek way and walked out of the building to my car. I learned three months later that he was Mr. Weckler—the owner of the Weckler Building and a guy worth about four million—but by that time I had forgotten the secret.

I drove back to my old office building and went in. In the lobby, I bought an early edition of the afternoon paper from one of the machines and carried it back to my office. When I got good and settled behind my desk with some whiskey, I went through the paper looking for articles on Mrs. Dyer's death. I scanned the front section and saw nothing. But in one of the back sections I located a small article telling how the police had found the body of an unidentified woman in a city park. They gave a short description of the deceased and asked for the public's cooperation in identifying her. I hoped they wouldn't get it.

I was very tired and my head ached. I downed another three pony glasses of whiskey for the pain—and for the frustration—but it didn't make me any less tired. I began to look through the rest of the paper just to have something to do. When I got bored, I walked over to the sofa and lay down.

That fairy tale is right. It is very pleasant to be wakened by a kiss. Her lips were cool and moist, her hair perfumed.

"That's the last time I wake a sleeping beauty," she said. "It smells like you've been sleeping with a bottle."

I opened my eyes and found Robert Grey's secretary standing over me. She was as pretty as ever, but her hair had been messed by the wind. I said:

"No, you just smell my French cologne."

"I think Scotch cologne would be more exact, but I'm not one to argue. Tell me, why are you sleeping on the job anyway? Aren't you afraid some of your 'friends' will come up here and do you in while you snooze?"

"They could, it's true. But none of them hate me enough to come to this part of town to do it."

"I think you have a point there."

"Then what are you doing here? And how did you find my office?"

"You sure ask a lot of questions."

"That's my job—when I'm not sleeping."

She motioned with her hand for me to scoot over and sat down next to me on the sofa. "Well, if you ever make enough money at your job to buy a new couch, I suggest you do it. This one is terrible. Anyway, I got your address from that dog-eared business card you gave me yesterday. And I came here to help you, believe it or not. I heard you and Mr. Grey yelling at each other today before I went on my break, so I figured you didn't get too far with him. I might be able to tell you a few things you don't know."

I looked into her eyes and smiled. They were light blue and mischievous looking. I had a feeling she was the type of person who never took anything too seriously. I said, "I'm sure you could tell me a lot of things I don't know, but why would you want to? Aren't you supposed to be loyal to Mr. Grey? He doesn't like anything told to seedy private investigators like me."

"My loyalty stops when my employment does. I don't work for Mr. Grey anymore. He got angry with me for typing a letter wrong, so he called the secretary service I work for to get a new girl. You see, I was only a temporary replacement while his regular secretary was on vacation."

"So your motive is revenge."

"Nope. I typed the letter wrong on purpose because I was tired of working there. I only take those jobs from the temporary service when I'm not modeling. Modeling is my main source of income."

"I can believe that. You still haven't told me why you drove all the way out here, though."

"A person sure has to go through a lot just to give you a little help," she said. "But I'll tell you anyway. I came out here because I like you and because I wanted to see a real private eye in action."

I winced. "There's no such thing as private eyes. Not anymore, at least. They went out with big-time gangsters and Bogey movies. The only people left in the business are the big boys with the electronic spy equipment and the little operators like me. I'm doing well if I gross a thousand bucks a month, and the jobs I get are always leftovers. This isn't a glamorous profession, and you can't make it that way by calling me a private eye. If you call me anything, please call me a private investigator."

She smiled. "Okay, Mr. Private Investigator, I came to see you in action. What exciting things have you done today besides sleeping?"

Nothing from my little speech had sunk in. She still expected me to talk out of the side of my mouth and show her the real brass knuckles I used to beat up criminals. I sighed. "Oh, not much. I did dispose of a body I found in the backseat of my car. And, of course, it's always exciting to sit with you on the same sofa."

"You're not making a comparison between the two events I hope."

"Never. Now tell me what I'm supposed to call you. I don't know your name."

"It's Lynn Marrow. I know yours is August from your card."

"All right, Lynn, let's go somewhere we can talk and maybe eat something decent at the same time."

We ate dinner at a nice restaurant and went back to her apartment, where I stole a few kisses. Much of the stuff she told me about Grey was useless. In her effort to play private eye with me, she blew the normal events of the office out of proportion. But there was one thing I found interesting: a tall man with a red, acne-scared face had come to Grey's office after I'd left. He'd argued with Grey for a while and then stormed out of the office, promising loudly that he would come to see Grey again this evening. Finally, something was clicking. I decided Grey and Pockface would have one more person at their meeting—me.

I parked my crate outside Grey's apartment building and went up the walk to the lobby entrance. The door was locked. It was on one of those intercom systems where you buzz up to the apartment to be let in. I punched about six of the room buttons and said "It's me, honey, I forgot my key" into the speaker as they answered. I got in on the fourth try.

Grey's apartment number, I knew from Delbert, was 312. I rode the elevator to the third floor and stepped out into a hallway that was as quiet as a sneak thief in the duchess's bedroom. I found the apartment on the right side and put my ear to it. I heard nothing. I reached for the doorknob, turned it slowly.

The knob twisted sharply in my hand. Somebody pulled the door open and my arm went with it. "Too bad for you, Hammond," said a voice. There was a swishing noise then, and I felt something burn hard at my left temple. Points of light blazed like welding sparks in front of my eyes. The floor reached up to grab me.

It was a man. He was saying something at my face, but I wasn't listening. He was tall—or he seemed to be at the angle from which I viewed him. He had black greasy hair and sideburns that were much too long. He smoked a huge cigar that looked and smelled like a smoldering road flare. It made me nauseous. His fat belly was like nine pounds of stuff in a five pound bag. Presently, he laughed at me and showed off a set of teeth that could have made a poor orthodontist very happy.

I blinked my eyes with pain and concentrated on coming back to life. I was lying on a sofa in the middle of a dark-paneled room. Dark pieces of matching furniture were scattered about the room on top of a dark brown carpet. Everything was dark. There were three men in the room—and at least one gun.

"This bird ain't too smart, is he, Mr. Mendoza?" Pockface said to the man with the cigar. Pockface gestured with his gun where he stood by the door, facing me. "He drives up to the apartment building and parks his car right underneath our window. Then he comes up to the apartment and expects to walk right in. Only thing is, he takes three weeks opening the door, and we have plenty of time to bash him in the head with a sap. You'd think he'd learn something gettin' bashed in the head all the time like he does."

"Yeah, you would, Eddie," said Mr. Mendoza. "Just like you'd think fat Mr. Grey over here would learn that it's not a good idea to back out of any deals he makes with me." Mendoza nodded at Robert Grey, who stood by the foot of the couch looking as white as a sheet from an operating table. "Do you think you know what I'm talking about, shamus?" Mendoza said to me.

I struggled to sit up. "Yeah," I said. "You helped

Grey and Pamela Dyer fake the theft of the pendant so you could fence it. You would get part of the money from the pendant for your trouble, and they would get the rest plus the insurance money. But they never came across with the pendant, so you're upset."

"That's close, shamus; you're smarter than I thought you were," said Mendoza. "You're right about everything except the part about Grey and Dyer not coming across with the pendant. That's not right; Mr. Grey gave us the pendant tonight. Look." Mendoza reached into his breast pocket and pulled out a gold, heart-shaped pendant on a fine chain. He dangled it in front of my face. It was exactly as Mrs. Dyer had described it—except there wasn't a large diamond at the top cleft, just a large hole. "So you see," Mendoza went on, "I'm not upset because they didn't give me the pendant. I'm upset because they didn't give me *all* of the pendant. Without the big rock, it's not even worth twenty grand: small change. And I don't deal for small change."

Robert Grey made a noise in his throat. His eyes became wide, and he looked at Mendoza with a pleading expression. He said, "But, Mr. Mendoza, I've already told you what happened to the large diamond. Pamela kept it. I told her you would be angry, but she wouldn't listen to reason. You must go and talk to her if you want the diamond."

I started laughing. My laughter filled the dark room with a strange sound. Three dumb faces stared at me.

"Stop it," ordered Mendoza.

I didn't.

Mendoza jerked his head at Eddie, who came up from the door. Eddie switched his gun to his left hand and hit me in the mouth with his right. I tasted blood immediately, and my laughing stopped. Then I laughed some more. "Again," said Mendoza. Eddie took a good swing this time and knocked me prone onto the couch. Blood flowed into my mouth.

"What's so funny, shamus?" Mendoza asked.

I looked up at Mendoza and felt cold hatred. "You should know," I said through thick, numb lips. "Ask your gunboy about last night."

Mendoza looked over at Eddie, but Eddie just shook his head. "Make it plain, Hammond," said Mendoza.

"Pamela Dyer is dead," I said for the third time today. "Eddie strangled her after they knocked me out. Then he dumped her in the backseat of my car, where I found her this morning."

Eddie shook his head furiously. "No, Mr. Mendoza, I didn't do anything like that. When I left the house last night, Mrs. Dyer was plenty alive."

I sat upright again and looked over at Grey. He was as nervous as a squirrel. "Sorry, Eddie, my mistake," I said. "You didn't kill Pamela Dyer; Grey did. I joked about it when I went to see him this afternoon, but now I see I was right. He must have come to the house after you left to pressure Mrs. Dyer into turning over the pendant." I turned to Mendoza. "That was the same reason you sent Eddie over there for, wasn't it? Mrs. Dyer was holding out."

Mendoza nodded.

"Well," I said, "Grey figured he and Pamela Dyer

couldn't afford to hold out against you, so he went to see her himself. That's when she told him she was keeping the big diamond. Grey must have gone berserk: he knew you wouldn't stand for it. He strangled her and took what was left of the pendant with him as a peace offering. He put Mrs. Dyer's body in my car because he wanted to frame me for the job, or he figured I would get rid of the body. Just like I did.

"There was only one problem. The maid at Mrs. Dyer's house saw the whole thing before she went home last night. That, or Grey thought she did. He went over to her house this afternoon to talk to her about it, but I showed up while he was there. He panicked again. After I left, he smashed the maid's skull with the rolling pin she'd been using in the kitchen. When I bumbled in a final time, he was forced to take a swing at me too. With me lying on the floor next to the body, he called the police and left in a hurry." I addressed Grey. "I bet you were pretty surprised when I showed up at your office right on your heels."

Things happened. Grey yelled something I didn't understand and dove at me on the couch. Eddie tried to block him, but the fat man's momentum was too much for Eddie. They both hit the couch, one on top of the other. I crawled over to them and made a play for Eddie's gun; this time I got hold of it. Mendoza made a move with his hand toward his jacket. Too bad for him. The gun jolted and three slugs found their way into his gut. Mendoza dropped to the floor, his skull making a thud as it hit. I giggled.

Eddie and Grey hesitated for a moment and then reached to restrain me. Too bad for them. I worked the trigger quickly. Two bullets slammed into Eddie's red face. The blood splattered on my arms and the couch. I turned the gun on Grey and fired. He slumped on top of my legs, died. I giggled some more.

I threw Grey's body off me and stood up. Blood was everywhere in the dark room. I looked down at the bodies and leered obscenely. I wasn't human.

My head was reeling, and I began to feel very, very sick. I went to the toilet and threw up. I phoned the police then.

The police really put me through the works. They didn't like the dead bodies on the apartment floor; they didn't like the missing diamond that they never found; they didn't like my running from the maid's house; they didn't like the way I moved Pamela Dyer's body; and most of all, they didn't like me. I didn't blame them. I was released after a seventy-two-hour confinement on suspicion of murder because of lack of evidence.

I quit then. I gave up. I stopped trying to be the clever private detective with all the witty chatter. I had had enough of the mindless killing, the low-class punks, and the high-class chislers I had to deal with, and the general feeling of cheapness. I was tired of being everyone's lackey. Give it to Hammond; he can take it. He loves being smacked in the head or punched around. Go ahead, hit him some more. He's tough. Yeah, he's tough—but not tough enough.

Delbert was horrified with the way things turned out. He couldn't accept the fact that I had killed three people. When I told him I was quitting, he offered me a job selling insurance with his company. I thanked him, but I wasn't ready to go that far in the other direction.

I saw Lynn Marrow a couple of times more, but her attraction to me wore off when she finally realized I was never going to work as a private detective again. It wasn't my fault. I had warned her once—once when I didn't realize how right I was: there's no such thing as private eyes.

Pincushion

DAVID A. BOWMAN

David A. Bowman describes himself as "just a regular guy" who likes good fiction—Jim Harrison and Jonathan Valin in particular—and has been practicing for ten years to write it. "Pincushion" is his first published story, if you don't count "The Big Nap," a mystery for young readers on computer diskette distributed by Scholastic Software, where he works as an editor. Mr. Bowman is presently at work on a private-eye novel. He is twenty-eight.

THE WOMAN showed up at his door with a Great Dane taller than a bicycle.

"Mrs. Rhine, please leave your friend outside," Foy Laneer said, trying to smile.

She let go of the dog's leash and it plowed past Foy's belly to the middle of the office, where it thumped down on the rug and began panting.

Mrs. Rhine edged past Foy and sat down on the

chair beside his desk. She was not a small woman. He could imagine her scooping mashed potatoes onto trays in a cafeteria.

Foy sat down behind his desk and asked Mrs. Rhine why she wanted to hire him to follow her husband.

"I think my husband is doing adultery again," she said, dropping her hands into her lap.

Foy got out a legal pad and pen to take notes. Mrs. Rhine told him that her husband was never at his office Tuesday and Thursday afternoons when he was supposed to be. She kept track of the daily mileage on his Impala. On those days he was driving 120 extra miles.

"Maybe he's out on business," Foy suggested with a shrug.

"He's doing adultery," Mrs. Rhine repeated.

She elaborated on her husband's history of infidelity. He noticed that her fingers were stained with what looked like ink from a black Magic Marker.

"If you had proof your husband was seeing another woman again, what would you do?" Foy asked.

"M.Y.O.B.," Mrs. Rhine replied. "You just find out where he does it and who he is doing it with."

Foy hated working for fruitcakes, but he got out a client form for her to sign. Suddenly, he noticed the Great Dane staring at him with such intense concentration that Foy felt like he was floating across the rug, moving closer and closer to the animal's face. He was conscious of a hollow space the size of an egg growing in the middle of his skull. He found himself loping across a field of wet grass, his ears perked up and snout pointed straight.

Then Mrs. Rhine started shaking his arm. He rubbed his eyes and said, "Do you have a photograph of your husband?"

As he heard her rummage in her purse, he looked at the dog sleeping on the floor and waited for the space inside his head to close up. Foy occasionally had what he called "out of the body" experiences. The best thing to do when they ended was concentrate on the business at hand. Mrs. Rhine handed him a Polaroid that had been taken at a wedding. The groom looked like a thug despite his tuxedo. Mrs. Rhine had been a slender bride and would have looked pretty except her lips were stretched in a lurid grimace. Based on her hairdo, Foy estimated they had been married about seven years.

"I'll start working on Tuesday."

"Start now," she whined.

"Your husband does driving on Tuesdays and Thursdays. Today is Friday."

She started to pout, so Foy told her how much two days of investigation would cost. She fished for her checkbook. Her purse was filled with black Magic Markers and a large notepad covered with scrawled hieroglyphics. The only word Foy could make out was "Jesus," and it appeared several times.

She gave him a check, then left, dragging the Great Dane behind her. The air in the office smelled like unwashed dog. Foy turned off the air conditioner and opened the windows. He saw Mrs. Rhine driving away in a station wagon filled with dogs. As she ran a red light, Foy wondered why Mr. Rhine walked down the aisle with her in the first place.

Foy made several phone calls. He found out that Mr. Rhine (Rocky Jay to his friends) was, in fact, a thug. He had been indicted on a narcotics charge, beat the rap at trial, but had served six months for possession of a sawed-off shotgun.

He opened a file drawer filled with road maps and pulled one out at random. He needed to relax, so he studied the forks of the freeways. Foy believed if a client was worried enough about his or her spouse to come to a private investigator, the odds were 99.9 percent in favor of adultery. The chances were good that Foy would hand Mrs. Rhine a report that reflected poorly on her husband's fidelity. She would tell Rocky Jay that she had hired a private investigator. Rocky Jay might then try to fix Foy's wagon.

Foy felt nervous but decided to live with the feeling until he knew what Rocky Jay was up to. He had been involved in a violent confrontation only once in his career. One night, Foy was photographing a couple dancing to the radio on the woman's patio. When she went into the house for more beer, the man heard Foy in the bushes and came running up holding a garden hoe over his head. Foy ducked, then grabbed the man by the collar and waltzed him in circles through the backyard, slapping the guy's face until he heard the crack of jawbone. The guy crawled away and Foy sat on the picnic table hyperventilating. Never before had Foy had such a sense of his own physical presence. He summoned up this memory whenever any redneck was giving him a hard time, and they always backed down.

Foy folded up the road map and turned the air conditioner back on.

On Tuesday morning Foy ate breakfast at the counter of a Lil' Chicken. He was across the street from Rocky Jay's office at the Hi-Ho Dogfood Company—a two-story factory building underneath a dull green water tower. He made small talk with the countergirls. They couldn't have been older than seventeen. When Foy rolled up his sleeves they asked where they could get tattoos like his. Foy thought that was cute, until he realized they weren't putting him on.

A little before noon, Rocky Jay stepped out of the building. Foy paid his tab and trotted to his car. Rocky got into a maroon Impala and drove out of the parking lot.

Foy turned his tape player on and it immediately started eating the tape. His radio had been stolen, so he had to content himself with just humming as he followed the Impala. Rocky Jay drove past the truck depots where the curbs were filled with rotted vegetables, then turned onto the interstate which cut through the immense cabbage farms that surrounded the city. Soon he was driving past Bible billboards and gas stations that sold bait, ice, and ammo.

Foy figured if Rocky drove 120 miles every Tuesday afternoon, they'd be stopping soon. They were heading for hill country when Foy saw the spire of a rocket ship on the horizon. Small bucket seats were twirling around the nose cone. Rocky Jay pulled into the huge gravel parking lot of Tornado County Amusement Park.

It was late August and the parking lot was jammed. After Foy parked, he sat until Rocky walked to the front gate, then he followed. The cars at the far end of the lot shimmered in the heat waves.

Foy paid the admission and got his hand stamped with orange ink. He waded through a swarm of waist-high kids, their fathers all bare chested with T-shirts tucked into waistbands. Foy noted some interesting knife scars.

Foy had been to Disneyland, so he was spoiled as far as amusement parks were concerned. He went there with his ex-wife and his stepkids and never had so much fun in his life. They rode a train and saw dinosaurs. He whipped down an artificial white mountain so fast he felt pulled inside out.

Foy pushed through the line for the Tilt-o-Whirl that snaked around the garbage cans and followed Rocky to a second ticket booth under a sign that said "To Enter You Must Be 21 or Over AND PROVE IT." Rocky Jay paid and entered. Foy reached the gate and got his hand stamped again, this time with green ink.

Inside, he walked past trailers covered with billboard-sized paintings that looked as if they were painted by giant psychotic children. He passed the "House of Human Reptiles" and "The Sleeping Nubian Princess." He passed an open-air tent where a sickly dwarf with no teeth sat at a miniature drum set and muttered. Foy figured any second now he would bump into a bearded lady.

Rocky Jay walked to a cinder-block bunker with a sign outside that said "The Pussykat Klub." Foy paused. The place was small and he didn't want to blow his cover, but he took a chance and entered.

The dim room smelled of bug spray. Foy almost tripped over the folding chairs. There was a wooden platform at the rear where a cone of cigarette smoke drifted under the single spotlight. The only other illumination came from a Coke machine.

The room could hold maybe fifty people; about twenty-five seats were taken. Rocky sat off to the side, stage right. Foy sat in the back row. Nothing happened for a while. Then a jaundiced man in a T-shirt brought a boom box up to the stage and turned it on. Incoherent funk blared for several minutes. When it was over, the yellowed man returned to the stage and said, "Gentlemen, please welcome Wanda Laneer!"

Foy Laneer jerked up. This was a county with a lot of Laneers in the phone book, and many of them were kin. He racked his brain but couldn't think of a relative named Wanda.

She was slim with heavy breasts, bouncing up to the stage wearing an Aladdin's Lamp getup of baby blue chiffon—the kind of pajamas a girl would pack for her honeymoon. Wanda ceremoniously placed an ivory box the size of a Kleenex dispenser on a card table, then bent over and stuck a cassette in the tape recorder.

She did a snaky belly dance to a top-ten pop song.

Little by little she unfastened parts of her pajamas and they fell around her ankles. She was young and didn't look real used. Her skin was clean and flushed, as if she had just stepped out of a hot bath.

She opened the ivory box and one by one removed long silver-colored needles and pushed them into her skin.

Foy knew of acupuncture, but he didn't believe what he was seeing. Soon Wanda was stuck with dozens of metallic quills that shimmered in the spotlight.

The men in the audience filled the room with a collective energy that made Foy again feel that he was running across the wet grass. When the tape finished, Wanda started pulling the needles out with smooth precision. Foy left.

Outside, the sunlight was a blunt glare. A number of beefy men with tattoos were hanging around. Foy rolled up his sleeves.

"The freak show over?" one of the guys asked him.

Foy shrugged. "Almost, I think."

Foy stood at the edge of the crowd next to a sausage stand. Eavesdropping, he found out that after Wanda's human-pincushion act there was a more conventional bump-and-grind show. The air smelled like frying grease, and listening to the sausage sizzle was as soothing as the sound of rain.

Soon after, Rocky filed out of the building in a group of men in rumpled sports jackets. They all looked glazed and sweaty. Foy trailed behind as they left the adult section of the amusement park. Rocky Jay headed for the parking lot.

Foy's car was an oven full of flies. As he cranked down the windows, he realized he'd left the wind-wing open. He started his car and followed Rocky back to the city.

On Wednesday morning, Mrs. Rhine appeared at his office door with the dog. He grabbed the dog's collar as it trotted into the office. The dog twisted its neck and put Foy's wrist into its mouth, holding it as gently as would a bird dog. The dog's snoot was the size of a loaf of bread. Foy let go of the collar.

"Buster is high strung," Mrs. Rhine said, as the dog flopped to the floor.

Foy shut the door. He sat at his desk and told Mrs. Rhine what he had observed on Tuesday. As he spoke, she couldn't take her eyes off the ink stamps on his hand. At the point he described Wanda's act, Mrs. Rhine started to bleat, "She sticks herself with needles? You are telling me sickness!"

Foy heard a sound like fish being beaten against a rock. He leaned over his desk and saw Mrs. Rhine pounding her fists against her thighs. As she jerked her head back and forth, she said, "I know she does the thing with him. You follow him and get me photographs. You do that tomorrow."

Foy tried to explain that all Rocky Jay did was watch. Mrs. Rhine sank down into the chair and balled up her face like she was crying. She didn't make a sound, and no tears fell.

Foy wanted to say, "There, there . . . ," but didn't have the energy. The Great Dane got up from the middle of the floor and trotted to the window. He stood up, put his front paws on the sill, and looked outside.

The next morning, Foy was parked near the dog-food company watching the drizzle. His tape player was fixed and he sang along with Crystal Gayle. She was singing a song about a lighthouse.

Rocky Jay left work in his car at 10:05 with Foy tailing him. They drove to Tornado County Amusement Park and ran across the parking lot in the rain to get their hands stamped.

In the cinder-block bunker, Rocky and Foy caught the tail end of an uninspired strip performed by a woman who looked like she had lived the wrong way for quite some time.

Foy saw some trucker types in the audience, but most of the men were the same ones who had been there on Tuesday. He had a hunch Wanda Laneer was going to stick needles into herself again.

Wanda hopped onto the stage dressed in a scarlet kimono. She held the gown closed as she bent over to drop a cassette in the tape player. The rock song sounded like something rolling around inside a cement mixer.

Wanda revealed herself quickly and shuffled geisha-like while flailing her arms in heavy-metal abandon. She gave a sly smile as she removed the first silver needle from the box.

Foy's pulse started to race, and his spine felt like a carrot that had just been pulled out of the dirt. He had to stand up and wait outside.

That night, Foy climbed up to the attic crawl space in his house. He searched with a flashlight and found a box of old books. He spent a few hours reading the Bible his mother had given him. He thought he remembered something about silver needles in the Old Testament. He paged through the Bible but had no luck. Two nights later he awoke thinking he heard an animal panting in the middle of his bedroom. He snapped on the light, but the room was empty.

On Monday he drove out to Tornado County by himself, playing his Crystal Gayle tape. When he stepped into the Pussykat Klub, he sat closer to the stage. He looked at the back of his hand and it resembled a passport. He heard the regulars sitting down behind him but didn't turn around.

For the Monday performance, Wanda wore an Egyptian robe of purple silk and a headdress like Nefertiti's. She had a thick gold band around her neck and wore several rings that looked like bits of jeweled seashells. She had black designs painted around her eyes. Wanda popped a cassette into the boom box and Foy's mouth dropped open when Crystal Gayle started singing the same song she had sung with him that morning.

As Wanda danced like an Egyptian princess, Foy sang along very quietly. Wanda looked him square in the eyes and he knew she was performing for him.

When her robe fell, he saw how creamy her skin was. There were no pock marks or scars from the needles. A drunk in the back of the bunker, started clapping, and yelled, "Come on, baby! Get hot!"

Five men quickly stood up and faced him. The drunk looked them over; when his eyes landed on Foy, he staggered up and left.

Wanda used twenty-three needles. Each one went through her skin as smoothly as if her flesh was butter. She held her head very erect. Foy thought she looked regal. The spotlight caused the needles to cast geometric shadows across her flesh. As she danced, the patterns moved like the spokes of a bicycle.

When Wanda removed the needles, Foy felt he had never seen a woman look as naked—not because of her physical nudity, but because the needles were no longer a part of her skin. Foy's tongue was raw from rubbing it against his front teeth. It felt like he'd been breathing through a spout at the top of his head.

As he left the bunker, the four other men who had stood up to the drunk each gave Foy a nod.

He leaned against the building for a moment to get his breath back. Then he snuck around to the back of the bunker. He saw Wanda getting into the cab of a pickup truck. Her hair was piled up on her head, and she would have looked like a Gibson girl except for the Cleopatra eye makeup. She started the truck and drove away.

Foy sprinted to the parking lot. If he was lucky, the pickup would have to leave through the parking lot.

He started up his car and waited. Just when he had given up hope, the pickup drove by. He backed out of his space and followed.

They drove down the interstate for about five miles until the truck pulled into the parking lot of a Red Rooster Motor Lodge. Wanda rolled up both windows before she got out. Foy pulled into the motel parking lot just as Wanda danced up the steps to the second landing and entered a room. Foy parked next to the fence that surrounded the swimming pool. He got out of the car and strolled to the soda machine, casing the motel.

Before he could return to his car, Wanda skipped back down the steps. She'd cleaned her face. She was wearing a low-back, one-piece bathing suit that was royal blue. Unlatching the fence gate, she walked across the sidewalk that surrounded the small rectangular pool. The cement must have been hot, because she started running on tiptoe to the edge of the water and dove in. From his angle, Foy couldn't see her and assumed she was swimming underwater. He tried to make it back to his car, but suddenly she surfaced in the shallow end and waved at him, yelling, "Hey, you there! Hey, shy boy!"

Foy walked over to the pool gate and leaned against the fence.

"Well, say hello or something," Wanda said, looking up at him. When Foy didn't answer, she added, "I noticed you today. You're the singer."

He said, "My name is Foy Laneer, and I wondered if we are related."

Wanda squinted and thought. They compared notes for several minutes until it was decided they weren't kin. Wanda looked angelic standing in the turquoise light of the pool. Foy looked at her body in the swimming suit, the image rippling in the water, and he couldn't believe that he had seen her do the things she had done. Now she possessed the same wholesomeness he'd seen in perky young gymnasts, the ones interviewed on "Wide World of Sports."

Foy heard footsteps and turned. A gray-haired man who looked like he was made from slabs of sunburned beef slowly walked to the pool gate.

"Wanda, finish your laps," the man said. "I've got to vacuum the pool."

"All right," Wanda said and then looked at Foy. "That's my brother-in-law, Kit. This is his Red Rooster."

Foy watched the man walk away and thought he should clear out. Kit would probably come back with guard dogs who were fed on raw meat and gunpowder.

"Well, it's been nice talking to you, Wanda," Foy said. "I really liked the music you played today."

Wanda smiled and began singing the song, and Foy joined in. While they sang, separated by a fence and ten feet of cement, Foy ran a brief home movie in his head of Wanda sitting in his lap, the two of them riding a little train through the Disneyland landscape of dinosaurs.

When they finished the song, Wanda climbed out of the pool and stood there dripping on the cement. Foy looked around for something that she could dry herself with. At that moment, he couldn't bear the sight of her standing there so wet.

"How come it doesn't hurt you to stick yourself with needles?" Foy asked.

Wanda shrugged. "It's like a gift. When I was nine years old, my daddy came back from Tucson and in the back of his pickup was this piece of cactus he lopped off in the desert. I planted it in a clay pot and put it on my windowsill."

A wasp flew by her head and she brushed it away. "One night, I had this bad dream. There was a big eye staring at me from the middle of the cactus."

She walked toward Foy and he opened the gate for her. She looked him in the eye and the water kept dripping off her. Foy tried to smile and looked around because he thought he heard dogs coming.

"In the morning," she continued, "a flower had bloomed on the cactus. I grabbed the pot and ran to show my daddy. I tripped and fell face first onto the cactus. It didn't hurt. That's when I knew I was gifted."

Then Wanda stuck her fingers under the material around her hips. "Do you like my bathing suit? This is my one special treat. Every year I get the most expensive bathing suit in the catalog. You wouldn't think a little piece of cloth would cost three weeks' salary, would you?"

Foy shook his head as Wanda danced past him, whipping drops of water from her hair across his face. She ran up the steps to her room and left the door open. Several seconds later, he saw her two hands extend out of the doorway and squeeze out the bathing suit in the walkway. He looked at the wet footprints on the stairs and followed them up toward the now empty doorway.

On Tuesday morning, Mrs. Rhine showed up at his office door, the four-pawed monster standing beside her.

"Where have you been?" she yelled. "I've been calling you for days and days."

Foy shrugged. "I had business. I followed your husband on Thursday. All he did was watch the girlie show and drive away."

Mrs. Rhine and the dog plowed into Foy's office. Foy left the door standing open and walked to the middle of the room.

"You take me out there," Mrs. Rhine screamed. "I'll fix her! She's hexed my husband. She won't sin anymore. No, no, no!"

He pointed at Mrs. Rhine and said, "There's nothing going on between the dancer and your husband."

Mrs. Rhine walked up to him and shook his shoulders, her belly bumping his. It felt like a hard mattress. "Don't you tell me that," she said. "I know what kind of man my husband is. You take me out there."

"Stop it," Foy said, grabbing wrists. Today her hands were covered with green Magic Marker ink. He looked over his shoulder to see if the dog was going to attack. The dog was staring transfixed at a mounted steelhead hanging on the wall.

Mrs. Rhine pulled away from Foy, with tears streaming down her face. "You don't understand. He made me do those things and my family found out and my church found out and now he's all I have left."

Foy felt bad for her, but in a detached way—as if she was a character on some TV show. Mrs. Rhine ran out the door.

"Hey, take the dog," Foy yelled. He grabbed the Great Dane's collar. The heavy dog was passive as it was dragged out the door and down the hallway to the front of the building. Foy saw Mrs. Rhine starting up her station wagon. The dog suddenly jerked its head and Foy lost his balance, falling to his knees. The Great Dane stared down at him and Foy felt the wet grass beneath his knees, the dog's face growing closer and closer until Foy passed into the dog's skull and through it. He was a dog, then a man again, and the next thing he saw was the Great Dane running away behind the Piggly Wiggly across the street.

Foy heard Mrs. Rhine drive away. He walked back to his office, locked it, and went to his car. "It's not over until the fat lady sings," Foy muttered as he drove to the dogfood company.

As he turned the corner, Rocky Jay passed him going in the opposite direction. Mrs. Rhine's station wagon followed several cars behind, a dozen dogs sticking their heads out of the windows. Foy made a sharp U-turn and followed.

Mrs. Rhine did an excellent job of tailing Rocky Jay. She stayed three car lengths behind, and if Rocky Jay knew his wife was following him, he wasn't letting on.

There was road construction on the way to Tornado County, and Foy lost track of them. When he finally pulled into the parking lot, Rocky Jay's Impala was already parked and empty. Foy parked across from the Impala, beside Mrs. Rhine's station wagon. The windows were rolled up all the way, and the panting dogs inside were in danger of suffocating.

Foy wondered if it was too late to stop Mrs. Rhine. Rocky Jay could fend for himself, but he didn't want Wanda to get hurt. Suddenly, a radar went off inside him and he ducked under the dashboard. He waited a few seconds and looked up. Two guys had walked past his car. One was a kid in a Harley Davidson T-shirt and dirty jeans that hung too low on his hips. The other was middle-aged and stocky. He was wearing a baseball jacket, and even at fifty feet Foy could tell the guy carried a gun under his arm.

The two stood by the trunk of Rocky Jay's car and scanned the parking lot. The stocky man gave a signal. A white van drove up. The kid opened the back door of the van. The stocky man opened Rocky Jay's trunk and yanked out two suitcases that were on top of the spare tire. He threw the suitcases into the back of the van. The kid pulled a canvas bag out of the van and threw it into Rocky Jay's car, slamming the trunk closed. The two men disappeared among the parked cars. The van sped away. The whole thing took twenty seconds.

Foy rested his head on the wheel. No one was going to give him the Sherlock Holmes of the Year award. He now realized Rocky Jay was doing weekly errands for the big boys. He'd drive his car out to the parking lot to make the switch. Maybe watching Wanda dance was part of the deal. Maybe someone in the audience was supposed to make sure Rocky Jay wasn't near his car to pull a double cross or something.

The way things stood now, Foy was sure Mrs. Rhine would cause a scene. Rocky Jay would know he'd been followed. He'd find out about Foy. Rocky Jay's friends would find out about Foy. Things didn't look so good.

Now Foy had to get to Mrs. Rhine before she did something stupid. He stepped out of his car and saw it was too late. Rocky Jay calmly walked across the parking lot to unlock his car. When he noticed his wife's station wagon, he frantically looked around. He whipped open the door and jumped in his car. Gunning the engine, he sped out of his parking slot throwing gravel.

Rocky drove past Mrs. Rhine as she marched out of the amusement park. She screamed and ran toward her car, her body in a crouch as if she were a hunchback. She opened the door into the side of Foy's car. A terrier jumped out and ran away. Mrs. Rhine backed her station wagon into a Toyota, then put it in drive and floored it.

Foy couldn't think of anything better to do, so he followed.

The Impala was at the exit. Foy heard the metallic crunch of Mrs. Rhine slamming her station wagon into the rear of Rocky Jay's car. The impact pushed him out into traffic, and he almost sideswiped a livestock truck full of cattle. He swerved just in time, then straightened with Mrs. Rhine tailgating right behind. Foy followed, amazed that they all didn't end up as steak on the highway.

Mrs. Rhine's station wagon wove across the dividing line as they sped down the two-lane that wound through the foothills. Foy could hear her pounding her horn. He saw the two cars take a sharp right turn bumper-to-bumper and disappear behind a hill. When Foy made the turn, Rocky Jay's car was suspended in midair. Foy blinked, then saw the car flipping over the trees. He skidded to a stop on the shoulder.

Mrs. Rhine's brakes screeched ahead of him. She jumped out of the station wagon, leaving the door open, and ran across the road to edge of the ridge. Dogs piled out of her car, scuttling across the highway in all directions. It looked like a scene from "The Little Rascals" where the dogs all escape from the dogcatcher.

Foy had to get out of there. He drove past as Mrs. Rhine was waving her arms, and the Doppler effect distorted her screaming. He swerved to avoid hitting some dogs. A mile down the road, he changed his mind and made a U-turn, putting his foot to the floor. He almost hit Mrs. Rhine as she ran back across the road to her station wagon. She tore away and dogs swarmed under the trees.

Foy jumped out of his car. He heard a diesel climbing the hill. He froze, then kicked at his tires until the truck passed. He made his way down the ridge and saw Rocky Jay's car wrapped around a pine. As he walked under the tree, something dripped on him. He looked up and saw Rocky Jay curled in the branches like a human bird nest.

Foy went to what was left of the back of the car. He tried the trunk, but it wouldn't budge, so he got a crowbar from his car to open it. He lugged the canvas bag up the hill, thinking it would be bad luck to open it now.

"The way things are going," Foy said to a mongrel who had run up to sniff his leg, "I'm probably either carrying Rocky Jay's laundry or a pipe bomb."

Foy's breathing didn't slow down until his car reached the interstate. If he had to put money on it, Foy would have bet the bag was filled with dope. He wanted to make a ceremony out of opening it—maybe have a beer first. Instead, he steered with his left hand and opened the bag with his right.

It was full of money. He almost plowed into the back of a semi. It was ridiculous trying to drive and count money at the same time, so he pulled off the road. When he was done counting the money, he spread a road map in his lap and thought. There were times in his life when he deserved a heavenly reward, but this wasn't one of them. He had been thick and had gotten a man killed, and now he was sitting beside a bag full of $300,000 in cash.

When the sun set, he drove to the Red Rooster Motor Lodge. The pool was a luminous lime wedge glowing from the underwater headlights. Foy didn't see Wanda's truck in the parking lot. A lumpy family was unloading their camper, and he helped the father carry a cooler full of rattling ice up the stairs to their room.

Foy walked back to Wanda's door and knocked. When there was no answer, he slipped inside. Her bathing suit was hanging over the bathtub, and he rubbed it against his face. He sat on her bed in the dark and waited. He heard the TV go on next door. Hours later he heard it go off. He got up and turned on the desk lamp. He got out a piece of motel stationery and realized he hadn't written a letter to a girl since he was in the service. He wrote a short note telling her he was leaving the city, and he would probably never see her again. Then he folded the note around a wad of approximately $50,000 and slid it under her pillow.

Just before he left, he noticed a metallic jar sitting by the TV. He took off the lid and it was full of silver needles buried in coarse black sand.

Foy drove to his office and cleaned out his file cabinets. There had been no mention of the accident on the radio news. Foy knew his biggest worry wasn't whether Mrs. Rhine gave his name to the police, but whether she gave his name to the two guys who put the canvas bag in Rocky Jay's trunk.

He went home and packed all his family pictures into a box. He carried them and his office files out to the barbecue pit on the patio and started a fire.

Foy cocked his head and listened past the crackling fire. He heard the distant zap of a bug light. He realized he was listening for Wanda. If she ever came to him, she would walk to his front door in the middle of the night and ring the doorbell. Suddenly, he heard branches cracking in the bushes. At the edge of the yard a huge animal stared at him. He heard the animal panting, its red eyes reflecting the fire. Then the animal turned and ran back into the darkness.

Psychodrama
MIKE HANDLEY

Mike Handley characterizes his mystery fiction as "eccentric hard-boiled." He has been a professional writer for five years, writing mystery fiction and contemporary horror stories, mostly for small-press magazines. He cites film noir as a primary influence on his work and has tried his hand at teleplays. He is currently working on a feature-length horror filmplay and a mystery novel.

"Psychodrama" is a fictionalized version of a holdup that occurred in Oakland, California, in August 1983. Mr. Handley has written a teleplay from the story.

HEY, LET ME TELL YOU, it started out playin' like the dream come true, I mean, blueprint beau-tiful, textbook perfect. I was thinkin' we were ready to talk Major Method, give workshops and whatnot.

We'd parked a street away where we could see the station across this rubbled lot. I was wheelin', Oakly sittin' shotgun. He had what he called "No Wave" music goin' in the tape deck, which he was usin' to psych up on, real militant stuff, all axe-edge rhythm and ambulance melody that shot straight to the nervous system, even at low volume.

We let the sun set so the night could work for us, sure, for cover and all that, but the way we were playin' it, atmosphere was one more factor to be exploited in our favor.

"Let's do it!" Oak snarled.

See, we always diced at the beginnin' to cast the main role, and Oak had won this round, so he was directin' the stop and go signs.

So I took the cue and rolled us around to Shelburne and on into the station, pullin' it up in front of the full-service pumps, right next to the office. Oak he jumped out and met the attendant in the doorway, just a kid, sixteen or so, you know the type, gone a little goofy over some certain flag twirler from school he can't get outa his head, standin' there all gangly in this greasy uniform with his name sewn over the pocket, Biff, or Buddy, or somethin'.

Well, Oak he slips the blade outa his sleeve and puts on his best crazy face. Let me tell you it was most effective. When the face was on him, he looked like nobody you'd ever want to see, 'cept maybe in a B movie where you could watch him terrorize somebody else.

I'd seen him back off this grizzly biker one night in a bar and once even a trio of Street Beaters, a much-feared local teen gang, real id kids, who'da just as soon as doused us with fuel and warmed their hands on our fire as wear gloves. But when the Oak flashed the face, flarin' the nostrils, bulgin' big with the eyes, showin' his teeth, well, it's just like they say, don't nobody mess with a crazy man!

And this kid, he knew that immediately. He must've just hit the bathroom 'cause he showed all the symptoms but the wet pants. Oak filled his fist with green and was back in less than a minute. I threw it in gear and gunned it, spinnin' the wheels purely for the sound effect.

It was that easy; a finger-snap green-light grab, hit and run without even a blow thrown, just bluff and burn 'em!

See? That's all it was. Sure it was still a heist, a criminal act, I ain't denyin' that. What I'm sayin' here is that we were doin' some street theater, fuckin' performance art!

What the Method was, was this. It wasn't no strongarm at all; it was nuthin' but acting all the way, technique and talent right there on the line. That blade? Strictly a prop, like they use on TV. Any pressure on the blade pushes it back in the handle, not an ounce of deadly force involved at all, pure psychodrama. And Oak had pulled off an Oscar's worth of performance; it was up to me to pull off the getaway.

And I was doin' just that, takin' time for a quick look in the mirror to admire the roll of rubber smoke and hopin' to catch the expression on the kid's face. But he was yellin' an' pointin' at us to some guy who'd just pulled up in a car.

I accelerated us outa there across two lanes of traffic, whippin' a one-hand ninety-degree right that triggered a three-car fender smash.

"You see that car?" I asked the Oak. "Think it's a cop?"

"XLM 846?"

"Didn't catch the plates." That Oak, he'd detail ya to death.

"You just didn't look. That's it all right, and he's comin' after us!"

If I could've zagged a quick left at the next corner I'd've lost him for sure, but I knew it was a wrong-way street so I punched it for the next block. The light blinked red. There were cars blockin' both lanes. Before I could get out an' pass 'em on the right this sporty lookin' foreign job carryin' some pretty boy and the dream girl of his choice pulls up to my bumper and I was boxed.

Suddenly the dude in the car appears right next to us and jumps out.

Oak hit the lock as the light turned green.

But this guy, hey, he was red, glowin' in the dark, screamin' somethin' that didn't sound like any words I know.

"Who the fuck is that?" I yelled, hittin' the pedal hard, then slammin' the brakes to keep from runnin' up the rear of the Gray Panther in front of me who was travelin' her own sweet pace.

"It's the owner! The fuckin' station owner!"

The shrill of his voice made me look over at the

Oak. Hey, he was truly spooked, retreatin' across the seat toward me.

That guy's face was fillin' the window; he was runnin' right along with us, five maybe ten miles an hour, even swung his fist against the window, but the safety glass held. Well, that was all the encouragement I needed. I swung the car over, forcin' him outa the way, then gunned it into that lane.

"He'd've shot me! If he'd had a gun, he'd a shot me! I'd be splashed all over you!" Oak was bawlin'. "That face! You see that face!"

I'd seen it all right, this guy'd gone bent round the bend, stark blazin' berserk. This was crazy incarnate! If he'd been a dog, they'd've shot 'im on the spot.

I was tryin' to weave us a way outa there, but the traffic was all clogged.

"How much we get?" I asked Oak, to get his mind off the immediate for a minute.

The money was still in his hand and he was turned around on his knees lookin' out the back. "I don't know."

"Well, why doncha count it. I'll keep an eye on him."

"You just get us outa here!"

Well now, I was doin' the best, believe me. I took an alley detour that got us into a side street that was just as jammed. There musta been some disaster around there somewhere and all the vehicles were gettin' funneled into this one area.

"A hundred and eighty-four." Oak called out.

That guy was still doggin' us. So far I'd been able to keep some cars between us, and I was thinkin' fast, rankin' our priorities in case the worst came and it got to be decision time. Survival of course took precedence. After all, the money wasn't the thing, strictly a small-time snatch, just icing. It was the act itself that was important, and the getaway.

That's when slow flow stopped up. The light had just gone green and I had got us almost all the way across the intersection, which left plenty of room for our two-car cushion to turn right to avoid the jam.

Well, that guy, he got himself a runnin' start and used our ass end to brake his momentum. The force impacted us into the car in front.

"Maybe if we refunded him half?"

"Give him all!" Oak screeched, shovin' the cash in my hand.

Well, I must confess, I did have to think about it, but I knew the whole instant that I had to do it; so I got out and started back toward him.

His car was stalled and a bit of smoke was leakin' out the hood. He was watchin' me with wide, almost all-white eyes, while grindin' 'way at the ignition.

Me I was makin' no sudden moves, keepin' the cash out there in fronta me like a shield. Trip this guy's wire and he'd go off in my face; so upon reachin' the door, I very carefully motioned for him to roll the window down.

He opened the door.

I had to kick it shut in my best firm but nonthreatenin' manner. Not an easy trick, in fact outright artful, but hey, for security's sake I wanted to keep at least that bit of barrier between us.

"No need to get out," I reassured him. "We deliver."

He was givin' me a real authentic-lookin' old-country evil eye.

I held the money to the glass. That got the window down.

"Here you go. It's all there, so just relax; everything is all right, justa simple mistake for which my friend and I offer our deepest heartfelt apologies."

Yeah, I know, it even sounded dumb in my ears, but shit, I didn't know what to say, and I don't think he was really hearin' me anyway.

So, I just made the switch without touchin' him. Whatever this creep had I certainly didn't want to catch.

He snatched it up and tried to get at me again.

Oak hit the horn, but I was already on the way with that loon on my tail. I leaped in the seat and threw the car in gear. Traffic was crawlin' forward, so I creeped away with it. That's all I could do, 'cept watch him get his car rollin' again right for us.

"Hold on." But Oak was already embracin' his seat. I read his face like a crossword puzzle, doom across the eyes and despair down the cheek. There was nuthin' reassuring I could say.

He hit us so hard my forehead bounced off the windshield. Oak tried to bail out then and there, but I got hold of his sleeve and held on.

Hey, I'da split myself, but you see, it was my car. We'd dressed it in hot plates, but it was still the only car I had. Couldn't just leave it there, and I was not about to stick it out by myself. I knew if things ever got down to the mano y mano with this maniac, we were gonna have to use tag-team tactics to survive. So I kept one hand clamped to the wheel, the other anchored to the ol' Oak.

"Lemme go!"

"Halfway home, pard, might as well ride it out."

Oak was squirmin' like a hooked fish outa water when we got hit yet again. It jerked the wheel right outa my hand and we jumped the curb, headin' right for this store window where I caught a fleeting glimpse of these well-formed female mannequins sportin' the latest in lacy bedwear.

It was only my sound instincts that kept my head clear of the panic, and I managed enough muscle control to steer us clear of the store and down the sidewalk into the alleyway and across, 'cause I just couldn't pull off the turn. So we hit the wall next door.

What can I say, the fuckin' physics was against me. I did what could be done, which was take the wheel in the gut.

I knew right away it was a sinkin' ship-type situation. We'd been truly torpedoed, and it was time for the rats to race the women and the children to the lifeboat. But hey, I was dazed to a glaze, fogbound in my body, treadin' the dark. I'm tellin' you, my head hurt one place, my body somewhere else.

Oak was yellin', and eventually it seemed I took

his advice and got my door locked before that guy could pull me outa the car.

He was jerkin' the handle and rockin' the whole car while I tried to get it started again, but it was like tryin' to raise the dead by telephone.

He suddenly turned and ran for his car. I tried to prepare myself for another rammin'. Through the window I could see a crowd was gatherin' to catch some on-the-spot entertainment.

He didn't disappoint them. He raced back to the door wavin' a tire iron which he wound up and swung smack into my window.

I couldn't believe it! The way this guy was actin' you'd a thought we'd kidnapped, raped, then murdered his wife, daughter, and dachshund! It was only money, fer Christ sakes!

So there I was, sunk so low I was actually hopin' somebody called the cops and they'd show up on cue like the cavalry, which they did.

I'll tell you, there's nuthin' worse than gettin' taught a painful lesson you learned thoroughly the first time. So let me be the voice of experience here for you and talk a little common sense, call it folk wisdom if you like. Just remember to remember, never mess with the crazy—whether man, woman, or animal.

And me? Just doin' my time, thinkin' of maybe writin' some plays. Believe me, from now on I'm confinin' my theater to the stage.

The Ripoff: Conclusion

JIM THOMPSON

Final installment. In the previous three installments Britt Rainstar's inability to act on his problems has made him the target of a series of murder attempts. His indecision has also resulted in promises to marry Manny Aloe (who is one of the murder suspects) and Kay Nolton (the police officer assigned to protect him), should he ever obtain a divorce from Connie.

24

IT WAS A pretty grim weekend.

Mrs. Olmstead decided to replace her usual grumbling and mumbling with silence—the kind in which conversation is omitted but not the clashing and crashing of pans, the smashing of dishes, and the like.

Kay performed her nurse's duties with a vengeance, taking my pulse and temperature every hour on the hour, or so it seemed to me, and generally interrupting me so often in doing her job that doing my own was virtually impossible.

Monday night, after dinner, there was a respite in the turmoil. Kay had retired to her room for a time, and Mrs. Olmstead was apparently doing something that could not be done noisily. At any rate, it seemed to be a good time to do some writing, and I dragged a chair up to my typewriter and went to work. Or, rather, I tried to. The weekend's incessant clatter and interruptions had gotten me so keyed up that I couldn't write a word.

I got up and paced around my office, then went back to my typewriter. I squirmed and fidgeted and stared helplessly at the paper. And, finally, I went out into the kitchen for a cup of coffee.

I shook the pot, discovering that there was still some in it. I put it on the stove to warm, and got a cup and saucer from the cupboard. Moving very quietly, to be sure. Keeping an eye on the door to Mrs. Olmstead's quarters and listening for any sounds that might signal a resumption of her racket.

I poured my coffee and sipped it standing by the stove, then quietly washed and dried the cup and saucer and returned them to the cupboard. And suddenly I found myself grimacing with irritation at the preposterousness of my situation.

This was *my* house. Kay and Mrs. Olmstead were working for *me*. Yet they had made nothing but trouble for me throughout the weekend, and they had certainly not refrained from throwing their weight around before then—forcing *me* to cater to *them*. And just why the hell should things be this way?

Why had most of my life been like this, a constant giving-in and knuckling-under to people who didn't give a damn about my welfare, regardless of what they professed or pretended?

I was brooding over the matter, silently swearing

that there were going to be some changes made, when I became aware of a very muted buzzing. So muted that I almost failed to hear it.

I looked around, listening, trying to locate the source of the sound. I looked down at the floor, saw the faint outline of the telephone cord extending along the baseboard of the cabinetwork. And I yanked open the door of the lower cupboard and snatched out the telephone.

Just as Manny was about to give up and hang up.

She asked me where in the world I'd been, and I said I'd been right there and I'd explain the delay in answering when I saw her. "But I'm sorry I kept you waiting. I wasn't expecting any calls tonight."

"I know, but I just had to call you, Britt. I've been reading the manuscript you gave me on erosion, and I think it's wonderful, darling! Absolutely beautiful! The parallel you draw between the decline of the soil and the deterioration of the people—the lowering of life expectancy and the incidence of serious disease. Britt, I can't tell you when I've been so excited about something!"

"Well, thank you," I said, grinning from ear to ear. "I'm very pleased that you like it."

"Oh, I do! In its own way, I think it's every bit as good as *Deserts on the March*."

I mumbled, pleased, saying nothing that made any sense, I'm sure. Even to be mentioned in the same breath with Dr. Paul Sears's classic work was overwhelming. And I knew that Manny wasn't simply buttering me up to make me feel good.

"There's only one thing wrong with what you've done," she went on. "It's far too good for us. You've got to make it into a full-length book that will reach the kind of audience it deserves."

"But PXA is paying for it. Paying very well, too."

"I know. But I'm sure something can be worked out with Pat. I'll talk to him after I talk to you, let's see, the day after tomorrow, isn't it?"

"That's right," I said.

"Well, I haven't read all you've done, and I want to read back through the whole manuscript before our meeting. So . . ." She hesitated. "I'm not sure I can make it on Tuesday. Suppose I call you Wednesday and see what we can set up?"

I said that was fine with me; I was glad to have the additional time to work. We talked a few minutes more, largely about the work and how well she liked it. Then we hung up, and I started to leave the kitchen. And Mrs. Olmstead's surly voice brought me to a halt.

"What's going on here, anyways? Wakin' folks up at this time o' night!"

Her face was sleep-puffed, her eyes streaked with threads of yellowish matter. She rubbed them with a grayish-looking fist, meanwhile surveying me sourly.

"Well?" she grunted, "I ast you a question, Mis-ter Rainstar."

"Hold out your hands," I said.

"Huh?" She blinked stupidly. "What for?"

"Hold them out! *Now!*"

She held them out. I put the phone in them, took her by the elbow, and hustled her out to the hallway writing desk. I took the phone out of her hands and placed it on the desk.

"Now that is where it belongs," I said, "and that is where I want it. Can you remember that, Mrs. Olmstead?"

She said surlily that she could. She could remember things a heck of a lot better than people who couldn't even remember to mail a letter.

"I tell you one thing, though. That phone's out here an' I'm back in the kitchen, I ain't sure I'm gonna hear it."

"All right," I said. "When you're actually in the kitchen working, you can keep the phone with you. But never put it away in a cupboard where I found it just now."

She shrugged, started to turn away without answering.

"One thing more," I said. "I've noticed that we're always running out of shopping money. No matter how much I leave for you, you use it. It's going to have to stop, Mrs. Olmstead."

"Now you listen to me," she said, shaking a belligerent finger at me: "I can't help it that groceries is high! I don't spend a nickel more for 'em than I have to."

I said I knew groceries were high. I also knew that Jack Daniels was high, and I'd noticed several bottles of it stowed in the bottom cupboard.

"You'll have to start drinking something cheaper," I said. "You apparently do a great deal of drinking in bars when you're supposedly out shopping, so I can't supply you with Jack Daniels for your home consumption."

She looked pretty woebegone at that, so I told her not to worry about it, for God's sake, and to go to bed and get a good night's sleep. And watching her trudge away, shoulders slumped, in her dirty old robe, I felt like nine kinds of a heel. Because, really, why fuss about a little booze if it made her feel good? At her age, with all passion spent and the capacity for all other good things gone, she surely was entitled to good booze. Drinking was probably all that made life-become-existence tolerable for her, as it probably is for all who drink.

I went to bed and to sleep. Thinking that the reason I hated getting tough with people was that it was too tough on me.

The next day went fairly well for me. There was practically no trouble from Mrs. Olmstead. I avoided any with Kay by simply submitting to her ministrations.

I got in a good day's work and continued to work until after nine that night.

Around ten, while I was toweling myself off after a shower, Kay came into the bathroom bearing a thermometer.

I took her by the shoulders, pushed her outside, and locked the door.

When I had finished drying myself, I put on my pajamas, came out of the bathroom, and climbed into bed, nodding at Kay, who stood waiting for me, prim-faced.

"Does that mean," she said icily, "that I now have your permission to take your temperature?"

"If you like," I said.

"Well, thank you so much!" she said.

She took my temperature. I held up my wrist, and she took my pulse, almost hurling my hand away from her when she had finished.

She left then, turning the light off and closing the door very gently. Some twenty minutes later, she tapped on the door with her fingernails, pushed it open, and came in. Through slitted eyes, I watched her approach my bed. A soft, sweet-smelling shadow in the dim glow of the hall light.

She stood looking down at me. Then her hands came out from behind her and went up over her head. And they were holding a long sharp knife.

I let out a wild yell, but the knife was already plunging downward.

It stabbed against my chest, then folded over as cardboard will. And Kay fell across me, shaking with laughter.

After a time, she crawled over into bed next to me, shedding her shorty nightgown en route. She nuzzled me and whispered naughtily in my ear. I told her she wasn't funny, dammit; she'd damned near scared me to death. She said she was terribly sorry, but she'd just had to snap me out of my stiffishness some way. And I said oh, well.

We were about to take it from there when I remembered something and sat up abruptly.

"My God!" I said. "You've got to get out of here!

This place is going to be full of cops in about a minute!"

"*What?* What the heck are you talking about?"

"The walls are bugged! Any loud cry for help will bring the police."

"Britt, darling," she said soothingly, "you just lie right back down here by mama. You just shut your mouth so mama can kiss it."

"But you don't understand, dammit! Jeff Claggett couldn't stake the place out, but I was afraid to come back here without plenty of protection. So—"

"So he told you that story," said Kay, and determinedly pulled me back down at her side. "And he gave you me. It's all the protection he could give you, and it's all you need. Take it from Officer Nolton, Britt. Soon-to-be-resigned Officer Nolton, thanks to your dear friend, the sergeant."

"Knock it off," I said crossly. "I had an idea all along that I was being kidded."

"Why, of course, you did," Kay said smoothly. "And, now, you're sure."

And now, of course, I was, since my yell for help had brought no response. Jeff had deceived me about the house being bugged, just as he had about Kay's status. He had done it in my own best interests, and I was hardly inclined to chide or reproach him.

Still, I couldn't help feeling that uneasiness which comes to one whose welfare is almost totally dependent upon another person, no matter how well intentioned that person may be. Nor could I help wondering whether there were other deceptions I didn't yet know about. Or whether something meant for my own good might turn out just the opposite.

25

My sense of uneasiness increased rather than diminished. It became so aggravated under Kay's incessant inquiries as to what was bothering me that I blew up and told her she was.

"Everything about you is getting to me," I said. "That blushing trick, the prudish-sweet manner, the cute-kiddy way you talk, like you wouldn't say crap if you were up to your collar in it, the —oh, crud to it!" I said. "You've got me so bollixed up I don't know what I'm saying anymore."

We were in my bedroom at the time—where else?— and I was fully prepared to go to bed—*by myself.*

Kay said she was sorry she got on my nerves, but I'd feel a lot better after I had something she had for me. She started to climb into bed with me. I put a leg up in the air, warding her off. She tried to come by the other way, and I stuck up an arm.

She frowned at me, hands on her hips. "Now, you see here, I have as much right to that bed as you have."

"Right to it?" I said. "You talk like a girl in a wooden hat, baby."

"You said you didn't think I was awful. Because I did it, I mean. You said you'd marry me if you weren't already married."

"Which I am," I said. "Don't forget that."

Kay said that part didn't matter. What was important was that I wanted to marry her, and that kind of made her my wife, and this was a community-property state, so half of the bed was hers. And while I was unraveling that one, she hopped over me and into bed.

I let her stay. For one thing, it is very hard to push a beautiful, well-built girl out of your bed. For another, while I knew she had skunked me again, that I had fallen for her act, it *was* a very good act. And what did one more fall matter to an incurable fall guy?

By the following day, Wednesday, my feelings of uneasiness had blossomed into a sense of foreboding. The feeling grew in me that things had gotten completely out of hand and were about to become worse and that there was nothing I could do about it.

It wasn't helped much by the bitter look Mrs. Olmstead gave me as she departed to do her shopping or drinking or whatever she did with my money. Nor was I cheered by a brief bit of sharpness that I had with Manny when she called to make an appointment with me. We finally made one for that afternoon, but I was still feeling quite down and more than a little irritated when Kay showed her into my office around four o'clock.

As it turned out, she also was not feeling her best, a fact she admitted as soon as our opening pleasantries were over.

"I don't want to argue with you, Britt," she said, "but you look quite well. I think you're probably in a lot better condition than I am. And as long as you've been going out, anyway—it isn't as if you were bedridden—I don't see why you couldn't have come to the office."

"Wait a minute," I said. "Hold it right there. Regardless of how well I look or don't look, I'm under strict orders not to leave the house."

"But I called here several times when you were out. At least Mrs. Olmstead told me you were. Of course . . ." Manny paused, frowning. "Of course, that could have been her way of saying that you just didn't want to talk to me . . ."

"There'd never be a time when I didn't want to talk to you. You should know that."

"I know. But . . ." She hesitated again. "Perhaps it wasn't Mrs. Olmstead. I thought it was, and she said it was but— Do you suppose it could have been what's-her-name, your nurse?"

"I'll find out," I said. "I know they've been feuding, and they just might have—one of them might have—tried to drag me into the quarrel." I pondered the matter a moment, then sighed and threw up my hands. "Hell, I'll never find out. Both of them are entirely capable of lying."

"Poor Britt." Manny laughed softly. "Well, it doesn't matter, dear. It doesn't bother me now that I know you haven't been going out at all."

"I haven't been. That's the truth, Manny."

"I believe you."

"The only time I've left the house was when I walked to your car with you last Friday."

"Well . . ." She smiled at me, her golden head tilted

to one side. "Since it's been so long, maybe you should walk to my car with me again today."

"Well . . ."

"Well?" Her smile faded, began to draw in around the edges. "You're afraid to, is that it? You still don't trust me."

"I haven't said that," I said. "You gave me your word that I had nothing more to fear from you, and I'm more than anxious to believe you. I could probably say something more positive if I wasn't a little bewildered."

"Yes? About what?"

"About your visit here this afternoon. I thought you were here to discuss my manuscript. But we've talked about practically nothing except my mishandled telephone calls and my walking to your car with you."

Manny's expression cleared, and she apologized hastily. "I'm sorry, dear. You have every right to be puzzled. But I like the manuscript better than ever, and Pat thinks it's a fine job too. He agrees that you should make a book out of it, and there won't be any problem about the money. We'll call it square for the right to do a digest."

"That's very generous of you," I said, "and I'm very grateful."

"We consider it a privilege to be associated with the project. I just wish I could be here to see it through to the end—not that you need my help, of course. But I can't be. T-that's w-why—" she averted her head suddenly. "That's why I made such a big thing of being outside the house with you. Even for a little while."

"I don't understand," I said. "What do you mean you can't be here until the work is finished?"

"I mean, this is the last time I'll see you. I'm leaving the company and going back East."

"B-but—" I stared at her, stunned. "But, why?"

"I'm getting married."

I continued to stare at her. I shook my head incredulously, unable to believe what I had heard.

"You're the only person I've told, so please keep it to yourself. I don't want anyone else to know just yet."

Married! My Manny getting married!

"But you can't!" I suddenly exploded. "I won't let you!"

"Oh?" She smiled at me sadly. "Why not, Britt?"

"Well, all right,' I said doggedly. "I can't marry you. Not now, anyway. Maybe never. But why the big hurry? We'd got everything straightened out between us, and I thought that—that—"

"That we could pick up where we left off? I'd've been willing to settle for that, at least until something better could be worked out. But it just isn't possible." She stood up and held out her hand. "Good-bye and good luck, Britt."

"Wait a minute." I also stood up, and I took her hand and held on to it. "Who is this guy anyway?"

"You wouldn't know him. I knew him in the East a long time ago."

"But why are you suddenly rushing into marriage with him?"

"Why do you think I'm rushing? But never mind. It's settled, Britt, so please let go of my hand."

I let go of it.

She turned toward the door, and I started to accompany her. But she gestured for me to remain where I was.

"I'm afraid I'm pretty stupid, darling. It's the police who've ordered you to stay in the house, isn't it? And your nurse is one of them?"

"Yes," I said. "To both questions."

"That's what Pat figured. He remembered her from somewhere, and it finally dawned on him that he'd seen her in uniform."

"All right," I said. "She's a cop, and I'm under orders not to leave the house. But I did it once, and since this is a pretty special occasion—the last time we'll see each other—"

"No!" she said sharply. "You'll stay inside as you've been told to!"

I said I'd at least walk to the front door with her, and I did. She held out her hand to me again, a firm little smile on her face, and I took it and pulled her into my arms. There was the briefest moment of resistance, then she came to me almost violently, as though swept on a wave of emotion. She embraced me, kissed me over and over, ran her soft, small hands through my hair.

And Kay Nolton cleared her throat noisily and said, "Well, excuse me!"

Manny drew away away from me, giving Kay an icy look. "How long were you watching us?" she demanded. "Or did you lose track of the time?"

"Never you mind, toots. I'm paid to watch people!"

"You should be paying," said Manny. "You get so much fun out of it."

And before Kay could come up with a retort, she was out of the house and slamming the door of the car. Kay said something obscene, then turned angrily on me. She said it was a darned good thing that Manny wasn't coming back to the house, and that she, Kay, would snatch her bald-headed if Manny ever did.

I accused her of snooping, listening outside the door while Manny and I were talking. She said I was doggone right she'd been listening, and if I didn't like it I could do the next best thing. I went into my office and closed the door, and at dinnertime she brought a tray in to me, also bringing a cup of coffee for herself.

She sat down across from me, sipping from her cup as I ate. I complimented her on the dinner, and made other small talk. In the midst of it she broke in with a curt question.

"Why isn't Miss Aloe coming here to the house anymore, Britt? I know she isn't, but I don't know why."

"You mean you missed part of our conversation?" I said.

"Answer me! I've got a right to know."

I lifted the tray from my lap and set it on a chair. I shook out my napkin and dropped it on top of the tray. Then I leaned back in my chair, and looked thoughtfully out the window.

"Well?" she said sullenly.

"I was just mulling over your remark," I said, "about your having a right to know. I don't feel that you have a right to know anything about my personal affairs. But I can see how you might, and I suppose it's my fault that you do. So, to answer your question: Miss Aloe is giving up her position here and going back East. That's why I won't be seeing her again."

Kay said "oh" in a rather timid tone. She said that she was sorry if she'd said or done anything that she shouldn't have.

I shook my head, brushing off her statement. Not trusting myself to speak. I was suddenly overwhelmed by my sense of loss, the knowledge of how much Manny had meant to me. And I jumped up and went over to the window. Stood there staring out into the gathering dusk.

Behind me, I heard Kay getting up quietly. I heard her pick up the dinner tray and leave the room, softly clicking the door shut behind her.

Several minutes passed. Then she knocked and came in again, carrying the phone on its long extension cord. She handed it to me and started to leave, but I motioned for her to remain. She did so, taking the chair she had occupied before.

"Britt?" It was Jeff Claggett. "How was your visit with Miss Aloe?"

"All right," I said. "At least partly all right. She's

leaving town and going back East. Yes, within the next day or so, I believe."

"The hell!" He grunted with surprise. "Just like that, huh? She give you any reason?"

"Well..." I hesitated. "I don't need to consult with her anymore. I'm going ahead with the work on my own."

"Yes? Nothing else?"

"I couldn't say," I said carefully. "What else could there be, and what does it matter, anyway? I am sure that I have nothing more to fear from her. I'm positive of it, Jeff. And that's all I'm concerned about."

"So who said no?" He sounded amused. "Why so emphatic?"

"Let it go," I said. "The point is that there's no longer any reason to continue our present arrangement. If you'd like to make it official, Miss Nolton is right here and—"

"Hold it! Hold it, Britt!" Claggett snapped. "I think we can close things out there very soon. But you leave it to me to say when, okay?"

"Well, all right," I said. "I think it would be better to—"

"Why guess about something when you can be sure? Why not wait until Miss Aloe actually leaves town?" He paused, then lowered his voice. "Nolton throwing her weight around? Is that it, Britt?"

"Well . . ." I sidled a glance at Kay. "I imagine it would be difficult to make a change, wouldn't it?"

"It would."

"All right, then," I said. "I'll manage."

We hung up, and I passed the phone back to Kay. She took it silently, but at the door she turned and gave me a stricken look.

I faced around to my typewriter and began pounding on the keys. And I kept at it until I was sure she had gone.

I had had about enough of Kay Nolton. What had started out as a pleasant giving, something that we could both enjoy, had wound up as an attempt to take me over.

I wasn't ready to be taken over, and I never would be. Nor would I ever want to take anyone else over. Love isn't tantamount to ownership. Love is being part of someone else, while still remaining yourself.

That was the way it had been with me and Manny. And now that she was gone from my life . . .

Well. Kay could not fill the space Manny had left. It was too great for any other to fill.

Kay left me alone that night. Which was just as well for her. I had discovered that confronting people when they insisted on it was not nearly so fearful as I had thought, and I was all ready to do it again.

The mood was with me the next day, and when Mrs. Olmstead appeared in my office doorway and announced that she needed more money to go shopping, I flatly refused to give her any.

"You've had far too much already," I told her coldly. "You've constantly emptied that cashbox in the telephone desk and then come grumbling to me for more. You must have had over six hundred dollars in less than two weeks' time. The best thing you can do now is to pack up your belongings and clear out."

"That don't make me mad none!" She glared at me defiantly. "You just pay me my wages, an' I'll be out of here faster'n you can say scat!"

"I don't have to pay you," I said. "You've already paid yourself several times over."

If she had given me any kind of argument, I probably would have relented. But surprisingly she didn't argue at all. Oh, she did a little under-the-breath cursing on her way out of my office. In no more than ten minutes, however, she was packed and gone from the house.

Kay, who had been standing by during the proceedings, declared that I had done exactly the right thing. "You should have done it long ago, Britt. You were far too patient with that woman."

"I've been that way with a lot of people," I said. "But it's a fault I'm going to correct."

She dropped her eyes, toeing in with one white shod foot, a slow blush spreading up her cheeks to blend with the auburn of her hair. It was all beautifully calculated. I have never seen such control. She was saying, as clearly as if she had spoken, that she had been a naughty, naughty girl and she was truly sorry for it.

"Will you forgive your naughty girl, Britt?" She spoke in a cute-child's voice. "She's awfully sorry, and she promises never to be naughty again."

"It doesn't matter," I said. "Forget it."

"Why, of course, it matters. But I'll be good from now on, honey. I swear I'll—"

"I don't care whether you are or not," I said. "I can hang by my thumbs a few days if I have to. If it takes any longer than that to wrap things up here, and if I still need a cop-nurse, you won't be her."

She gave me no more argument than Mrs. Olmstead had. I was amazed at how easy it was to tell people off—without being very proud of it—although, admittedly, my experience was pretty limited.

I didn't feel much like working; the thought of Manny, *my Manny*, being married to another was too much on my mind. But I worked, anyway, and I was still at it when Claggett arrived in midafternoon.

Manny was back in the hospital, he informed me. The same reputable hospital she had been in before with the same reputable doctors in attendance.

And, as before, she was in absolute seclusion, and no information about her condition or the nature of her illness was being given out.

26

"I could probably get a court order and find out," Claggett said, "if I could show any reason why it was necessary for me to know. But I can't think what the hell it would be."

"Probably there isn't any," I said. "Nothing sinister, I mean. She told me yesterday that she wasn't feeling well. Possibly she got to feeling worse and had to go to the hospital."

"Possibly. But why so secretive about it?"

"Well . . ."

"Tell you something," Claggett said. "Maybe I'm a little cynical, but I've never known anyone to pull a cover-up yet unless there was something to cover up."

"That's probably true. But this could hardly be called a cover-up, could it?"

"It's close enough. And the one thing I've found that's usually covered up with doctors is mental illness. It's my guess," said Claggett thoughtfully, "that Miss Aloe has had a nervous breakdown or something of the kind. The second one in less than a month. Either that or she's pretending to. So that leaves us with a couple of questions."

"Yes?" I said. "I mean, it does?"

"To take the last one first. If she's pretending, why is she? And, secondly, if she's actually had a nervous collapse, what brought it on?"

"I just hope she's all right," I said. "In any case, I don't see what her being in the hospital has to do with me."

"Well, it could be just a coincidence, but the last time she was hospitalized, you had a pretty bad accident."

"It *was* a coincidence," I said, and wondered why I suddenly felt so uncomfortable and uneasy. "I'm positive that she's leveling with me, Jeff. I knew it when she wasn't, and I know it now that she is."

Claggett shrugged and said that was good. He, himself, would never trust his own judgment where someone he loved was concerned. Because you could love someone who was completely no good and untrustworthy.

"But we'll see," he said, and stood up. "I have no basis for believing that she's not on the level with you, but we shouldn't be long in finding out."

I walked to the door with him, wondering whether I should tell him about Manny's impending marriage. But I had promised not to, and I could think of no reason why I should.

We shook hands, and he promised to keep in touch. Then, just as he was leaving, he abruptly pulled me back from the door and moved back into the shadows himself.

I started to ask what was the matter, but he gestured me to silence. So we stood there tensely in silence, waiting. And then there was the sound of footsteps mounting to the porch and crossing to the door.

My view was obscured by Jeff Claggett and the heavy shadows of the porch. But I could see a little, see that a man was standing with his face pressed against the screen to peer inside.

Apparently he also was having a problem in seeing, for he reached down to the door handle, pulled it open, and stepped uncertainly across the threshold.

Claggett grabbed him in a bone-crushing bear hug, pinning his arms to his sides. The man let out a startled gasp.

"W-what's going on here?"

"You tell me, you son of a bitch!" rasped Claggett. "Let's see how fast you can talk."

"It's all right, Jeff," I said. "He's my father-in-law."

27

Connie's letters to me had gone unanswered. When she telephoned, Mrs. Olmstead told her I had moved and that she had no idea where I was. And for the last ten days or so, the phone had simply gone unanswered. Luther Bannerman had determined to find out just what was what (to borrow his expression). And he'd driven all the way here from the Midwest to do it.

He was in the dining room now with Kay, stuffing himself with the impromptu meal she had prepared for him at my request, rambling and rumbling on endlessly about my general worthlessness.

". . . me an' daughter just couldn't support him any longer, so he comes back down here. An' he sent her a little money, but it was like pulling teeth to get it out of him. And this last month, more than a month, I guess, he didn't send nothing! No, sir, not one red cent! So I just up and decided—Pass me that coffeepot, will you, Miss. Yes, and I believe I'll have some more of them beans an' potato salad, and a few of them . . ."

In the kitchen, Jeff Claggett unwrapped the strip of black tape from around the telephone cord and held the two ends apart.

"A real sweet old lady," he laughed sourly. "Well, that takes care of any calls since she left today, if you had any since then. But I'm damned if if I understand how she could head off the others."

I said it was easy, as easy as it was for her to see that I got no mail that would reveal what she was up to. "She kept the phone out in the kitchen when she was in the house, and when she was away she hid it where it couldn't be heard."

"And you never caught on?" Claggett frowned. "She pulls this for almost a month, and you never tipped?"

"Why should I?" I said. "If someone like you called, of course, she'd see that you got through to me. Anyone else would be inclined to take her at her word. She had a little luck, I'll admit. But it wasn't all that hard to pull off with someone who gets and makes as few calls as I do."

"Yeah, well, let's get on with the rest of it," Claggett sighed. "I hate to ask, but. . . ?"

"The answer is yes to both questions," I said. "Mrs. Olmstead mailed the checks I sent to my wife—or rather, she didn't mail them. And she made my bank deposits for me—or didn't make them."

Claggett asked me if I hadn't gotten deposit slips, and I said no, but the amounts were noted in my bankbook. Claggett said he'd just bet they were, and he'd bet I hadn't written "For deposit only" on the back of the checks. I said I hadn't and couldn't.

"I needed some cash for household expenses," I explained, "and I'd run out of personal checks. I had some on order, but they never arrived."

"I wonder why." Claggett laughed shortly. "Well, I guess there's no way of knowing how much she's taken you for offhand or how much, if any, we can recover—when and if we catch up with her. But Mr. Blabbermouth, or Bannerman, shapes up to me like a guy who means to get money out of you right now."

"I'm sure of it," I said. "I should have at least a few hundred left in the bank, but it wouldn't be enough to get him off my back."

"No," he said. "With a guy like him there's never enough. Well—" he drew a glass of water from the sink, drank it down thoughtfully, "want me to handle him for you?"

"Well . . ." I hesitated. "How are you going to do it?"

"Yes or no, Britt."

I said yes. He said all right, then. *He* would do it, and there was to be no interference from me.

We went into the dining room and sat down across from Bannerman. He had stuffed his mouth so full that a slimy trickle streaked down from the corner of it. Claggett told him disgustedly to use his napkin, for God's sake. My father-in-law did so, but with a pious word of rebuke.

"Good men got good appetites, Mister Detective. Surest sign there is of a clean conscience. Like I was telling the young lady—"

"We heard what you told her," Claggett said coldly. "The kind of crap I'd expect from a pea-brain loudmouth. No, stick around, Nolton." He nodded to Kay, who resumed her chair. "I'd like to know what you think of this character."

"He already knows," Kay said. "I told him when he tried to give me a feel."

Bannerman spluttered red-faced that he'd done nothing of the kind. He'd just been tryin' to show his appreciation for all the trouble she'd gone to for him. But Kay had taken her cue from Claggett—that here was a guy who should have his ears pinned back. And she was more than ready to do the job.

"Are you calling me a liar, buster?" She gave him a pugnacious glare. "Well, are you?"

He said, "N-no, ma'am, 'course not. I was just—"

"Aaah, shut up!" she said.

And Claggett said, "Yes, shut up, Bannerman. You've been talking ever since you stepped through the door today, and now it's time you did some listening. You want to, or do you want trouble?"

"He wants trouble," Kay said.

"I don't neither!" Bannerman waved his hands a little wildly. "Britt, make these people stop—"

"All right, listen and listen good," Claggett said. "Mr. Rainstar has already given your daughter a great deal of money. I imagine he'll probably provide her with a little more when he's able to, which he isn't at present. Meanwhile, you can pack up that rattletrap heap you drove down here in and get the hell back where you came from."

Anger stained Luther Bannerman's face the color of eggplant. "I know what I can do all right!" he said hoarsely. "An' it's just what I'm gonna do! I'm gonna have Mr. Britton Rainstar in jail for the attempted murder of my daughter!"

"How are you going to do that?" Claggett asked. "You and your daughter are going to be in jail for the attempted murder of Mr. Rainstar."

"*W-what?*" Bannerman's mouth dropped open. "Why, that's crazy!"

"You hated his guts," Claggett continued evenly. "You'd convinced yourselves that he was a very bad man. By being different from you, by being poor instead of rich. So you tried to kill him, and here's how you went about it. . . ."

He proceeded to explain, despite Bannerman's repeated attempts to interrupt. Increasingly fearful and frantic attempts. And his explanation was so cool and persuasive that it was as though he was reciting an actual chronicle of events.

The steering apparatus of my car had been tampered with; also, probably, the accelerator. Evidence of the tampering would be destroyed, of course, when my car went over the cliff. All that was necessary then was for me to be literally driven out of the house, so angered that I would jump into the car and head for town.

But Connie had overdone the business of making me angry. She had pursued me to the kitchen door—and been knocked unconscious when I flung it open. And when I headed for town, she was in the car with me. . . .

"That's the way it was, wasn't it?" Claggett concluded. "You and your daughter tried to kill Mr. Rainstar, and your little plan backfired on you."

My father-in-law looked at Claggett helplessly. He looked at me, eyes welling piteously.

"Tell him, Britt. Tell him that Connie and me w-wouldn't, that we just ain't the kind of p-people to—to—"

He broke off, obviously—*very* obviously—overcome with emotion.

I wet my lips hesitantly. In spite of myself, I felt sorry for him. This man who had done so much to humiliate me, to make me feel small and worthless, now seemed very much that way himself. And I think I might have spoken up for him, despite a stern glance from Jeff Claggett. But my father-in-law compensated in blind doggedness for his considerable shortcomings in cerebral talents, and he was talking again before I had a chance to speak.

"I'll tell you what happened!" he said surlily. "That fella right there, that half-breed Injun, Britt Rainstar, tried to kill my daughter for her insurance! He stood to collect a couple of hundred thousand dollars, and that was just plenty of motive for a no-account loafer like him!"

Claggett appeared astonished. "You mean to tell me that Mr. Rainstar was your daughter's beneficiary?"

"Yes, he was! I'm in the insurance business, and I wrote the policy myself!"

"Well, I'll be damned!" Claggett said in a shocked voice. "Did you know about this, Britt?"

"I told you about it," I said, a little puzzled. "Don't you remember? Mr. Bannerman wrote up a similar policy on me with my wife as beneficiary, at the same time."

He nodded, and said "Oh, yes," it all came back to him now. "But the company rejected you, didn't they? They wouldn't approve of your policy."

"That's right. I don't know why exactly, but apparently I wasn't considered a very stable character or something of the kind."

"You were a danged poor risk, that's what!" Bannerman said grimly. "Just the kind of fella that would get himself in a fix with the law. Which is just what you went and done! Why, if I hadn't spoken up to the sheriff, after you tried to kill poor little Connie—"

He chopped the sentence off suddenly. He gulped painfully, as though swallowing something that had turned out to be much larger than he had thought.

Kay gave him a cold, narrow-eyed grin. There was a snap to Claggett's voice like a trap being sprung.

"So Mr. Rainstar was a pretty disreputable character, was he? *Was he, Bannerman?*"

"I—I—I didn't say that! I didn't say nothin' like that, a-tall, an' don't you—"

"Sure, you did. And you told everyone in town what a no-goodnik he was. A blabbermouth like you would be bound to tell 'em, and don't think I won't dig up the witnesses who'll swear that you did!"

"But I didn't mean nothin' by it. I was just talkin'," Bannerman whined. "You know how it is, Britt. You say you wish someone was dead, or you'd like to kill 'em, but—"

"No," I said. "I've never said anything like that in my life."

"You didn't trust your son-in-law, Bannerman," Claggett persisted. "And you sure as hell didn't like him. But you allowed the policy on your daughter to stand—a policy that made him her beneficiary? Why didn't you cancel it?"

"I— Never you mind!" Bannerman said peevishly. "None of your doggoned business, that's why!"

Claggett asked me if I had ever seen the policy, and I said I hadn't. He turned back to Bannerman, his eyes like blue ice.

"There isn't any policy, is there? There never was. It was just a gimmick to squeeze Mr. Rainstar. Something to threaten him with when he tried to get a divorce."

"That ain't so! There is too a policy!"

"All right. What's the name of the insurance company?"

"I—I disremember, offhand," Bannerman stammered, and then blurted out, "I don't have to tell you, anyway!"

"Now look, you!" Claggett leaned forward, jaw jutting. "Maybe you can throw your weight around with your friendly hometown sheriff. Maybe he thinks the sun rises and sets in your ass. But with me, you're just a pimple on the ass of progress. So you tell me: what's the name of the insurance company?"

"But I—I really don't—"

"All right." Claggett made motions of rising. "Don't tell me. I'll just check it out with the Underwriters Bureau."

And, at that, Bannerman gave up.

He admitted weakly that there was no policy and that there never had been. But he brazenly denied that he and Connie had done wrong by lying about it.

Ol' Britt was tryin' to get a divorce, and she had a right to keep him from it, any way she could. And never mind why she was so dead set against a divorce. A woman didn't have to explain a thing like that. The fact that she didn't want one was reason enough.

"Anyways, Connie hasn't been at all well since the accident. Taken all kinds of money to pervide for her. If she hadn't had some way of scarin' money out o' Britt—"

"Apparently, she's able to take care of herself now," Claggett said. "Or do you have round-the-clock nurses? And just remember I'll check up on your story!"

"Well . . ." Bannerman hesitated. "Yeah, Connie's coming along pretty good right now. Course, she's all jammed up inside, an' she's always gonna be an invalid—"

"What doctor told you that? What doctors? What hospital did her X rays?"

"Well . . . ," Bannerman said weakly. "Well . . ." and said no more.

"Jeff," I said. "Can't we wind this up? Just get this —this *thing* the hell out of here? If I have to look at him another minute, I'm going to throw up!"

Claggett said he felt the same way, and he jerked a

thumb at Bannerman and told him to beat it. The latter said he'd like to; there was nothing he'd like to do more. But he just didn't see how he could do it.

"I used practically every cent I had comin' down here. And that ol' car of mine ain't gonna go much farther, without some work bein' done on it. I *want* t'get back home; these here big cities ain't for me. But—"

"Save it," Claggett said curtly. "You've probably got half of the first nickel you ever made, but I'll give you a stake to get rid of you. Nolton." He gestured to Kay. "Get him in his car, and see that he stays in it till I come out."

"Yes, sir! Come on, you!"

She hustled my father-in-law out of the room, and the front door opened then closed behind them.

I gave Claggett my heartfelt thanks for the way he had handled things and promised to pay back whatever money he gave my father-in-law.

"No problem." He dismissed the matter. "But tell me, Britt. I was just bluffing, of course, trying to shake him up, but do you suppose he and your wife did try to kill you?"

"What for?" I said. "I was willing to get out of their lives. I still am. Why should they risk a murder rap just because they hated me?"

"Well, hatred has been the motive for a lot of murders."

"Not with people like them," I said. "Not unless it would make them something. I'll tell you, Jeff, I don't see them risking a nickel to see the Holy Ghost do a skirt dance."

He grinned. Then, again becoming thoughtful, he raised another question.

"Why is your wife so opposed to divorce, d'you suppose? I know you'll give her money as long as you have it to give, but—"

"Money doesn't seem to have anything to do with it," I said. "She was that way right from the beginning, when I didn't have a cent and it didn't look like I ever would have. I just don't know." I shook my head. "There was a little physical attraction between us at one time, *very* little. But that didn't last, and we never had any other interests in common."

"Well." Claggett shrugged. "Bannerman was right about one thing. A woman doesn't have to give a reason for *not* wanting a divorce."

We talked about other matters for a few minutes, i.e., Mrs. Olmstead, my work for PXA, and the prospects for suing over the condemnation of my land. Then he went back to Bannerman again, wondering why the latter had caved in so quickly when he, Claggett, had threatened to call the Underwriters Bureau.

"Why didn't he try to bluff it out, Britt? Just tell me to go ahead and check? He had nothing to lose by it, and I might have backed down."

"I don't know," I said. "Is it important?"

"We-el . . ." He hesitated, frowning. "Yes, I think it might be. And I think it bears on the reason for your wife's not giving you a divorce. Don't ask me why. It's just a hunch. But . . ."

His voice died away. I looked at his troubled face, and again I felt that icy tingling at my spine—a warning of impending doom. And even as he was rising to leave, a pall seemed to descend on the decaying elegance of the ancient Rainstar mansion.

28

Claggett drove off toward town to get some money for my father-in-law, Bannerman following him in his rattletrap old vehicle. Kay came back into the house.

While she prepared dinner for the two of us, I cleaned up the mess Luther Bannerman had left and carried the dishes out into the kitchen. She glanced at me as I took clean silver and plates from the cupboard, asked if I was still mad at her. I said I never had been—I'd simply tried to set her straight on where we stood. Moreover, I said, I was grateful to her for the several jolts she had given my father-in-law.

She said *that* had been a pleasure. "But if you're not mad, why do you look so funny, Britt? So kind of down-in-the-mouth?"

"Maybe it's because of seeing him," I said. "He always did depress me. On the other hand . . ."

I left the sentence hanging, unable to explain why I felt as I did, the all-pervading gloom that had settled over me. Kay said she was sort of down-in-the-dumps herself, for some reason.

"Maybe it's this darn old house," she said. "Just

staying inside here day after day. The ceilings are so high that you can hardly see them. The staircase goes up and up, and it's always dark and shadowy. You feel like you're climbing one of those mountains that are always covered with clouds. There are always a lot of funny noises, like someone was sneaking up behind you. And . . ."

I laughed, cutting her off. The house was home to me, and it had never struck me as being gloomy or depressing.

"We both need a good stiff drink," I said. "Hold the dinner a few minutes, and I'll do the honors."

I couldn't find any booze; Mrs. Olmstead apparently had finished it all off. But I dug up a bottle of pretty fair wine, and we had some before dinner and with it.

We ate and drank, and Kay asked how much Mrs. Olmstead had stolen from me. I said I would have to wait until tomorrow morning to find out.

"It really doesn't bother me a hell of a lot," I added. "If she hadn't gotten it, my wife would have."

"Oh, yes. She tore up the checks you sent your wife, didn't she?"

"That's right," I said.

"Well, uh, look, Britt . . ." She paused delicately. "I've got some money saved. Quite a bit, actually. So if you'd like to—"

I said, "Thanks, I appreciate the offer. But I can get by all right."

"Well, uh, yes. I suppose. But—" Another delicate pause. "How about your wife, Britt? How much do you think she'd want to give you a divorce?"

I told her to forget it. Connie had apparently made up her mind not to give me a divorce on any terms, and there was no use in discussing it.

"I don't know why. Perhaps she has a reason, and I'm too stupid to see it. But—" I laughed suddenly, then quickly apologized. "I'm sorry, Kay. I just thought of a story my great-grandfather used to tell me. Would you care to hear it?"

"I'd love to," she said, in a tone that gave the lie to her statement.

But I told it to her, anyway.

There was once a handsome young Indian chief who married a maiden from a neighboring tribe.

She was neither fair of figure or face, and her disposition was truly ugly. Never did she have a kind word to say to her husband. Never was he able to do anything that pleased her. She was simply a homely shrew, through and through. And the tribe's other squaws and braves wondered why they remained together as husband and wife.

The days passed, and the months, and the years.

Finally, when the chief was a very old man, he died.

His wife laughed joyously at his funeral, having inherited his many ponies and buffalo hides and other such wealth. And this, his wealth, was her reason, of course, for marrying him and remaining with him for so many years.

Kay stared at me, frowning. I looked at her deadpan, and she shook her head bewilderedly.

"That's the end of the story? What's the point?"

"I just told you," I said. "She married him and stuck with him for his dough. Or the Indian equivalent thereof."

"But—but, darn it! Why did he marry her?"

"Because he was stupid," I said. "His whole tribe was stupid."

"*Wha-aat?*"

"Why, sure," I said. "A lot of Indians are stupid. That's why we wound up in the shape we're in today."

Kay jumped up and left the table.

29

I was sorry now that I had told her the story, but it hadn't been a rib. My great-grandfather actually had told it to me, a bit of bitter fun-poking at Indians, their decline and fall. But there was wisdom in it for any race.

We all overlook the obvious.

Danger is so commonplace that we have become insensitive to it.

We wring the hand of Evil and are shocked at the loss of fingers.

I left the dining room, pausing in the hallway to glance into the kitchen. Kay was aware of me, I am sure, but she did not look up. So I went on down the hall to the vast reception area, crossed its gleaming parquet expanse, and started up the stairs.

It hadn't occurred to me before, but what Kay had said was true. The upward climb was seemingly interminable and as shadowed as it was long. There were those strange sounds, also, like stealthy footsteps in pursuit, sounds where there should have been none. And, due to a trick of acoustics, no sounds where sounds should have been.

I reached the landing, breathing hard, almost leaping up the last several steps. I whirled around, tensed, heart pounding. But there was no one behind me. Nothing but shadows. Cautiously, I looked down over the brief balustrade that joined the top of the staircase to the wall of the landing.

The parquet floor below me was so distant that I would not have known that it was there had I not known that it was, so distant and so cloaked in darkness. I backed away hastily, feeling more than a little dizzy.

I went on to my room, cursing my runaway imagination. Calling down curses upon Kay for her unwitting planting of fear in my mind. Cops should know better than that, I thought. It didn't bother cops to talk about darkness and shadows and funny noises, and people sneaking up behind other people. Cops were brave—which was not an adjective that could be applied to Britton Rainstar.

I was, at least figuratively, a very yellow red man.

I had a streak of snowy gray right down the middle of my raven locks. And I had a streak of another color right down the middle of my tawny back.

I got out of my clothes and took a shower.

I put on pajamas and a robe and carpet slippers.

My pulse was acting up, and there was a kind of

jumpiness to my toes. They kept jerking and squirming of their own volition; my toes always do that when I am very nervous. I almost called out to Kay when she came up the stairs, because she was a nurse, wasn't she? and I certainly needed something to soothe my nerves.

But she was miffed at me, or she would have come to me without being summoned. And if I managed to un-miff her, I was sure, what I would get to soothe me was Kay herself. One of the best little soothers in the world, but one that I simply could not partake of.

I had screwed the lid on that jar (you should excuse the expression). She was forever forbidden fruit, even though I should become one, God forbid.

I tried to concentrate on nonscary things. To think of something nice. And the nicest thing I could think of was something I had just determined not to think of. And while I was doing my damndest not to think of her, simultaneously doing my damndest to think of something else, she came into my room.

Fully dressed, even to her blue cape. Carrying her small nurse's kit in one hand, her suitcase in the other.

"All right, Britt," she said. "I'm moving in here with you or I'm moving out. *Leaving!* Right this minute."

"Oh, come off of it," I laughed. "You'd get a permanent black eye with the department. As big as your butt, baby! You'd never get a decent job anywhere."

"But you won't know about it, will you, Britt?" She gave me a spiteful grin. "After I leave, and you're all alone here in this big ol' house . . ."

She set her bags down and did a pantomime of what

would happen to me, clawing her hands and walking like a zombie. And it was ridiculous as hell, of course, but it was pretty darned scary too.

". . . then the big Black Thing will come out of the darkness," she intoned, in ghostly tones, "and poor little Britt won't see it until it's too late. He'll hear it, but he'll think it's just one of those noises he's always hearing. So he won't look around, and—"

"Now, knock it off, dammit!" I said. "You stop that, right now!"

". . . and the big Black Thing will come closer and closer." (*She came closer and closer.*) "And closer and closer, and closer—GOTCHA!"

"Yeow!" I yelled, my hair standing on end. "Get away from me, you crazy broad!"

"'Fraidy cat, 'fraidy cat!" she chanted. "B. R. has a yellow streak running down his spine!"

I said I'd rather have a yellow streak running down it than pimples. She said angrily that she didn't have pimples running down hers. And I said she would have when my hex went to work.

"A pretty sight you'll be when you start blushing. Your back will look like peaches flambé in eruption. Ah, Kay, baby," I said, "enough of this clowning around. Just give me something to make me sleep, and then go back to your room and—"

"I *won't* go back to my room! But I'll give you a hypo if you really want it."

"If I want it?" I said. "What do you mean by that?"

"I mean, I won't be here. You'll be aww-ll all-alone, with the big Black Things. I thought you might be afraid to go to sleep aww-ll all-alone in this big ol' house, but—"

"All right," I said grimly. "We wound up our little affair, and it's going to stay wound up. You know it's best for both of us. Why, goddammit—" I waved my arms wildly. "What kind of a cop are you anyway? A cop is supposed to be something pretty special!"

She said she was something pretty special, wasn't she?—managing a demure blush. I said she could stay or get out, just as she damned pleased.

"It's strictly up to you, Miss Misbegotten! My car keys are there in the top dresser drawer!"

"Thank you, but I'll walk, Mr. Mangy Mane. I'm a strong girl, and I'm not afraid of the dark."

She picked up her bags and left.

I heard the prolonged creaking of the stairs, as she descended them. A couple of moments later, I heard the loud slamming of the front door.

I settled back on the pillows, smugly grinning to myself. Dismissing the notion of going downstairs and setting the bolts on the door. It would be a lot of bother for nothing. I would just have to go down and unbolt it, when Kay came back. As, of course, she would in a very few minutes. Probably she had never left the porch.

I closed my eyes, forcing myself to relax. Ignoring the sibilant scratchings, the all-but-inaudible creakings and poppings peculiar to very old houses.

I thought of the stupid Indian and his blindness to the obvious. I thought of Connie's senseless refusal to give me a divorce. I thought of Luther Bannerman, his quick admission that Connie had no insurance policy when he thought Claggett was going to check on it.

Why didn't Connie want a divorce? Why the fear of Claggett's checking with the insurance company? What—

Oh, my God!

I sat up abruptly, slapping a hand to my forehead, wondering how I could have missed something that an idiot child should have seen.

I was insured. That was what Claggett would have discovered. Bannerman had lied in saying that the insurance company had rejected me.

Why had he lied? Why else but to keep me from becoming wary, to allay any nasty suspicions I might entertain about his and Connie's plans for me.

Of course, the existence of the policy would have to be revealed in order to collect the death benefit. The double-indemnity payoff of two hundred thousand dollars. But there was absolutely nothing to indicate that fraud and deception had been practiced to obtain the policy. Quite the contrary, in fact.

I, myself, had applied for it and named Connie as my beneficiary. She had what is legally known as an insurable interest in me. And if I was the kind of guy—as I provably was—who might neglect or forget to keep up my premium payments, she had the right to make them for me. Moreover, she definitely was not obligated to make the fact known that I had the policy, an asset that could be cashed in or encumbered to her disadvantage.

If her marital status should change, if, for example, we should be divorced, I would have to certify to the change. And, inevitably, I would actually know what I had only been assumed to know—that I *was* insured. So there could be no divorce.

Connie and her father couldn't risk another automobile accident by way of killing me. Two such accidents might make my insurers suspicious. An accident of any kind there on their home grounds might arouse suspicion, and so I had been allowed to clear out.

I returned to my home. After a time, I began remitting sizable sums of money to Connie, and as long as I did I was left alone. They could wait. Time enough to kill me when the flow of money to Connie stopped.

Now, it had stopped. So now—

A blast of cold air swept over me. The front door had opened. I sat up abruptly, the short hairs on my neck rising. I waited and listened, nerves tensing, face contorted into a stiffening mask of fear.

And then I grinned and relaxed, lay back down again.

It would be Kay, of course. I hadn't expected her to stay away this long. To say that I was damned glad she had returned was a gross understatement. But I must be very careful not to show it. Now, more than ever, Kay had to be kept at a distance.

After all, I had promised to marry her—when and if I was free. And Connie's attempt to murder me was a felony, noncontestable grounds for divorce.

Kay would undoubtedly hold me to my promise. Kay was a very stubborn and determined young woman. Once she got an idea in her head, she would not let go of it, even when it was in her own interests to do so. Maybe it was a characteristic of all blushing redheads. Maybe that was why they blushed.

At any rate, there must be no gladsome welcomes between us, nothing that might develop into intimacy.

Perhaps I should pretend to be asleep, yes? But yes. Definitely. It would show how little I was disturbed by her absence. It would throw figurative cold water on the hottest of hot-pantsed redheaded blushers.

I closed my eyes and composed myself. I folded my hands on my chest, began to breathe in even-measured breaths. *This should convince her,* I thought. *Lo, the Poor Indian, at rest after the day's travail. Poor Lo, sleeping the sleep of the just.*

Kay finished her ascent of the stairs.

She came to the door of my room and looked in at me.

I wondered how I looked, whether my hair was combed properly and whether any hair was sticking out of my nose. Nothing looks cruddier than protruding nose hairs. I didn't think I had any, but sometimes they show when you are lying down when they would not show otherwise.

Kay crossed to my bed, stood looking down at me. My nose twitched involuntarily.

She had apparently been running in her haste to get back to me. She had gotten herself all sweaty, anyway, and she stank like hell.

I am very sensitive about such things. I can endure

the direct hardships—my Indian heritage, I suppose. But I *can't* stand a stinky squaw.

I opened my eyes and frowned up at her.

"Look, baby," I said. "I don't want to hurt your feelings, but—b-bbbbbbb-uht—"

It wasn't Kay.

It wasn't anyone I had ever seen before.

30

He was a young man, younger than I was. I knew that without knowing exactly how I knew it. Perhaps it was due to cocksureness, the arrogance that emanated from him like the odor of sweat. He was also a pro—a professional killer.

No one but a pro would have had the incredible nervelessness and patience of this man. To loiter in a hospital lobby, say, until he could give me a murderous shove down its entrance steps. Or to wait in the fields adjacent to my house, until he could get me in the scope of his high-powered rifle. Or, missing me, to go on waiting until the house was unguarded and I was unprotected.

The pro knows that there is always a time to kill, if he will wait for it. He knows that when necessity demands disguise, it must be quickly and easily used, and readily disposed of. And this man was wearing makeup.

It was a dry kind, a sort of chalk. It could be applied with a few practiced touches, removed with a brush of the sleeve. I could detect it because he had overused it, making his face a shocking mask of hideousness.

Cavernous eyes. A goblin's mouth. Repulsively exaggerated nostrils.

And why? Why the desire to scare me witless? Hatred? Why would he hate me?

There was a *click*. The gleam of a razor-sharp switchblade. He held it up for me to see—gingerly tested its murderous edge, then looked at me grinning, relishing my stark terror.

Why? Who? Who could enjoy my torture, and why?

"Why, you son of a bitch!" I exploded. "You're Manny's husband!" His eyes flickered acknowledgment as I looked past him. "Get him, Manny! *Get him good, this time!*"

He turned his head. An impulse reaction.

The ruse bought me a split second. I vaulted over the end of the bed and hurtled into the bathroom, slammed and locked the door, just as he lunged against it.

A crack appeared in the inlaid paneling of the door. I called out to the guy shakily, foolishly. "I'm a historical monument, mister. This house is, I mean. You damage a historical monument, and—"

His shoulder hit the panel like a pile driver.

The crack became a split.

He swung viciously and his fist came through the wood. He fumbled blindly for the lock. I stooped, opened my mouth, and chomped down on his fingers.

There was an anguished yell. He jerked his hand back so hard that I bumped my head against the door. I massaged it carefully, listening, straining my ears for some indication of what the bastard would try next.

I couldn't hear anything. Not a damned thing.

I continued to listen, and I still heard nothing.

Had he given up? No way! Not so soon. Not a professional killer with a personal interest in wasting me. Who hated me, was jealous of me, because of Manny.

"Look, you!" I called to him. "It's all over between Manny and me. I mean it!"

I paused, listening.

"You hear me out there? It's you and her from now on. She told me so herself. Maybe you think she's stalling by going to the hospital, but . . ."

Maybe she was, too. Maybe her earlier hospitalization had also been a stall. Or maybe just the thought of being tied up with this guy again had driven her up the wall. Because he really had her on the spot, you know?

She had tried to kill him, had done such a job on him that she believed she *had* killed him. Thus her long convalescence after his "death." Also, after his recent reappearance, he would have discovered her painful pestering of me in the course of casing her situation. So she was vulnerable to pressure—a girl who had not only tried to kill her husband but had also pulled some pretty raw stuff on her whilom lover.

And the fact that her husband, the guy who was pressuring her, was on pretty shaky grounds himself would not deter him for a moment.

For he was one of those bullish, dog-in-the-manger types. The kind who would pull the temple down on his head to get a fly on the ceiling. That was the way it was. Add up everything that had happened and that was the answer.

I called out to him again, making my voice stern. I said I would give him until I counted to ten, wondering what the hell I was talking about. *Until I counted to ten, then what?* But he didn't seem very bright, either, so I went right ahead.

"One two three four—*Do you hear me? I'm counting!*—five six seven eight—*All right! Don't say I didn't warn you!*—ni-un ten!"

Silence.

Still silence.

Well, he could be gone, couldn't he? I'd chomped down on his fingers damned hard, and he could be seriously bitten. Maybe I'd even gotten an artery, and the bastard had beat it before he bled to death.

It just about had to be something like that. I would just about have to hear him if he still remained here.

I unlocked the door. I hesitated, then suddenly flung it open. And—

I think he must have been standing against the far wall of the bedroom. Nursing his injured hand. Measuring the distance to the bathroom door as he readied himself for the attack upon it.

Then, at last, hurtling himself forward. Head lowered, shoulders hunched, legs churning like pistons, rapidly gaining momentum until he hit the door with the impact of a charging bull. Rather, he *didn't* hit the door, since the door was no longer there. I had flung it open. Instead, he rocketed through the opening and hit the wall on the opposite side. And he hit it so hard that several of its tiles were loosened.

There was an explosive *spllaat*! He bounced backward, and his head struck the floor with the sound of a bursting melon.

For a moment, I thought he must be dead. Then, a kind of twitching shudder ran through his body, and I knew he was only dead to the world. Very unconscious, but very much alive.

I got busy.

I yanked off my robe and tied him up with its cord.

I grabbed up some towels and tied him up with them.

I tied him up with the hose of the enema.

I tied him up with the electric-light cords from the reading lamps. And some pillowcases and bedsheets. And a large roll of adhesive bandage.

That was about all I could find to tie him up with, so I let it go at that. But I still wasn't sure that it was enough. With a guy like that, you could never be sure.

I backed out of the bathroom, keeping my eye on him. I backed across the bedroom, still watching him, and out into the hallway. And then I stopped stock-still, my breath sucking in with shock.

Connie stood flattened against the wall, immediately outside my door. And lurking in the shadows at the top of the stairs was the hulking figure of my father-in-law, Luther Bannerman.

I looked from him to her, staring stupidly, momentarily paralyzed with shock. I thought, *How . . . why . . . what . . . ?* Immediately following it with the thought, *How silly can you get?*

She and Bannerman had journeyed from their home place together. Having a supposedly invalided daughter was a gimmick for chiseling money from me. So he had parked her before coming out to my house this afternoon, picking her up afterward. Since Kay wouldn't have volunteered any information, they assumed that she was no more than the nurse she appeared to be, one who went home at night. She left. While they waited to make sure she would not return, they saw Manny's husband enter the house in a way that no legitimate guest would. So they followed him inside, and when he failed to do the job he had come to . . .

My confusion lasted only a moment. It could have taken no longer than that to sort things out and put them in proper order. But Connie and Luther Bannerman were already edging toward me. Arms outspread to head off my escape.

I backed away. Back was the only way I could go.

"Get him, Papa!" Connie hissed. *"Now!"*

I saw a shadow upon the shadows—Bannerman poising to slug me. I threw up an arm, drew my own fist back.

"You hypocrite son of a bitch! You come any closer, I'll—!"

Connie slugged me in the stomach. She stiff-armed me under the chin.

I staggered backward and fell over the rail of the balustrade.

I went over it and down, my vision moving in a dizzying arc from beamed ceiling to paneled walls to parquet floor. I did a swift back-and-forth review of the floor and decided that I was in no hurry at all to get down to it.

I had never seen such a hard-looking floor.

I was only sixty-plus feet above it—*only!*—but it seemed like sixty miles.

I had hooked my feet through the balusters when I went over the rail.

Connie was alternately pounding on them and trying to pry them loose, meanwhile hollering to her father for help.

"Do something, darn it! Slug him!"

Bannerman moved down the stairs a step or two. He leaned over the rail, striking at me. I jabbed a finger in his eye.

He cursed and let out a howl.

Connie cursed, howled for him to do something, goddammit!

"Never mind your damned eye! Hit him, can't you?"

"Don't you cuss me, Daughter!" He leaned over the rail again. "It ain't nice to cuss your papa!"

Connie yelled "Oh, shit!" exasperatedly, and gave my foot an agonizing blow.

Her father took another swing at me, and my head seemed to explode. I heard him shout with triumph, Connie's maliciously delighted laugh.

"That almost got him, Papa. Just a little bit more now."

"Don't you worry, Daughter. Just you leave him to papa."

He aimed another blow at me. She hit my sore foot again.

And I kicked her, and I grabbed him.

He was off balance, leaning far out over the rail. I grabbed him by the ears, simultaneously kicking at Connie.

He came over the rail with a terrified howl, clutching my wrists for dear life. My foot went between Connie's legs, and she was propelled upward as Bannerman's weight yanked me downward.

She shrieked, one terror-filled shriek after another. Shrieking, she flattened herself against my leg and hung on to it.

She shrieked and screamed, and he yelled and howled. And one jerked one way, and the other pulled the other way. And I thought, *My God, they're going to deafen me and pull me apart at the same time.*

They were really a couple of lousy would-be murderers. But they were amateurs, of course, and even a pro can goof up. As witness, Manny's husband.

I caught a glimpse of him, as I was swung back and forth, looking more like a mummy than a man, due to the variety and number of items with which I had bound him. He came hopping through my bedroom door, very dazed and wobbly looking. He hopped out onto the landing, lost his balance, and crashed heavily into the balustrade.

It creaked and scraped ominously. The distant floor of the reception hall seemed to jump up at me a few inches, and the terrified vocalizings of the Bannermans increased.

Somehow, the mummy got to his feet again, though why I don't know. I doubt that he knew what he was doing. He got to the head of the stairs, stood looking down them dazedly. He executed another little hop—and, of course, he fell. Went down the steps in a series of bouncing somersaults, hitting the leg that Bannerman had just managed to hook over the rail.

The jolt almost knocked Bannerman loose from me. Naturally, I was yanked downward also, simultaneously exerting a tremendous yank upon the balustrade.

It was too much. Too damned much. It tore loose from its ancient moorings and dropped downward. Connie skidded down my body headfirst, unable to stop her plunge until she was extended almost the length of her body. Clutching her father's legs, she clung to me by her heels.

She screamed and cursed him, hysterically. He cursed and kicked at her.

A strange calm had settled over me—the calm of the doomed. I was at once a part of things and yet outside them, and my overall view was objective.

I didn't know how the few screws and spikes that still attached the balustrade to the landing managed to stay in place, why it didn't plunge downward, bearing us with it, into the reception hall. Moreover, I didn't seem to care. Rather, I cared *without* caring. What concerned me, in a vaguely humorous way, was the preposterous picture we must have made. Connie, Bannerman, and I balled together in a kind of crazy bomb, which was about to be dropped at any moment.

I waited for the weight to go off of me, the signal that we were making the final plunge. I waited, and I kept my eyes closed tight, knowing that if I opened them, if I looked down at that floor so far below me, it would be about the last time I looked at anything.

There was so much racket from the Bannermans and the grating and screeching of the balustrade that I could hear nothing else. But suddenly the weight did go off of me in two gentle yanks. There was another wait then, and I expected to hit the floor at any moment. Then, I myself was yanked, and a couple of strong arms went around me. And I was hustled effortlessly upward.

I was set down on my feet. I received a gentle bearing-down shake, then a sharp slap. I opened my eyes, found myself on the second-floor landing, with its ruined balustrade.

Connie and Bannerman were stretched out on the floor, facedown, with their hands behind their heads. Manny's husband lay at the foot of the stairs in a heap.

Kay peered at me anxiously. "I'm terribly, terribly sorry, darling. Are you all right?"

"Fine," I said. Because I was alive, wasn't I, and being alive was fine, wasn't it?

To show my gratitude, I would gladly have gone down on my knees and kissed her can.

"I would have been back sooner, Britt, but a truck driver tried to pick me up. I think I broke his darned jaw."

"Fine," I said.

"Britt, honey . . . we don't have to say anything to Sergeant Claggett about my leaving you alone, do we? Let's not, okay?"

"Fine," I said.

"I'll think of a good story to cover. Just leave it to me."

"Fine," I said.

"You do love me, don't you, Britt? You don't think I'm awful?"

"Fine," I said.

And then I put my arms around her and sank slowly down to my knees.

No, not to kiss her can, although I really wouldn't have minded.

It was just that I'd waited as long as I could—and I couldn't wait any longer—for something soft to faint on.

31

Kay's story was that she had gone out of the house to investigate some suspicious noises and had found a guy apparently trying to break in. During her pursuit of him (he had got away) Manny's husband and, subsequently, the Bannermans had entered the house. But, fortunately, she was in time to overpower them and save me from death.

The story didn't go down very well with Jeff Claggett, but he couldn't call her a liar without calling me one, so he let it go. And not only did Kay keep her job with the department, she received a commendation and promotion. The increase in pay, she estimated, would pay for the all-white gown and accoutrements. Which, she advised me unblushingly, she intended to wear at our wedding.

To move on:

Connie and Luther Bannerman pleaded guilty to attempted murder and conspiracy to commit murder. They received ten years on each count, said sentences to run consecutively.

Manny's husband remained mute and was convicted of attempted murder. But other charges were dug up against him before he could begin serving sentence—he was a very bad guy, seemingly. The last I heard, he had accumulated two life sentences, plus fifty years, and he was still standing mute. Apparently, he saw nothing to gain by talking.

Manny was taken from her hospital to the criminal ward of the county hospital. Pat Aloe could have got her out, I am sure, since the charge against her of harboring a criminal—failing to report her husband to the police—was a purely technical one. But Pat had grimly washed his hands of Manny. He wanted nothing more to do with her. He had no further need for her, for that matter, having begun the swift closing out of PXA's affairs.

Manny cooperated fully with the authorities, and their attitude toward her was generally sympathetic. She had attacked her husband without intent to kill him. His abuse had driven her temporarily insane, and when she recovered her senses, she was holding a steam pressing iron in her hand and he was sprawled on the ground at her feet. The storm was gathering by now, and she was forced to flee back inside her resort cabin. When the police came in the morning to investigate the storm's havoc, she was near death with shock and was never questioned about her husband's supposed death.

Actually, he wasn't even seriously hurt, but there was a dead man nearby—one of several who had died in the storm—who resembled him in size and coloring. Manny's husband made the features of the dead man unrecognizable with a few brutal blows, switched clothes with him, and planted his identification on him.

He disappeared into the night then, and no one ever questioned the fact that he was dead. Possibly because so many people were glad to have him that way. Rumors had been circulating for some time that he had irritated people who were not of a mind to put up with it, and only his apparent death saved him from the actuality.

There followed an extended period of hiding out, of keeping out of the way of former associates. Finally, however, believing that feeling about him had cooled down, and having sized up Manny's situation, he had paid her a covert visit.

She was terrified. Anyone who knew him well would be. Also, she was vulnerable to his threats, thanks to the nominal attempt on his life and the malicious mischief she had made for me. She couldn't go to the police. She couldn't go to Pat, who was already furious with her. So she acceded to her husband's demands. She would go away with him, if he would leave me alone.

She collapsed after his visit and was forced to go to the hospital. His reaction was to try to kill me. She hoped to buy him off, and he accepted the money she gave him. But, of course, he would not stay bought. Again, he gave her an ultimatum: She would go back to him, or I would go—period. So she had agreed to go back to him, but the ugly prospect had brought on another nervous collapse with its resultant hospitalization.

Actually, he had no intention of leaving me alone, regardless of what she did. He was a handsome hood, and as vain and mean as he was handsome. And it was simply not tolerable to him to allow his wife's lover to live.

So he had tried to kill me for the third time. At the same time the Bannermans were attempting to kill me for the second time. And so much for them.

The charge against Manny was dismissed, with the urgent recommendation that she seek psychiatric help. She gladly promised to do so.

Mrs. Olmstead was caught up with in Las Vegas. She was drunk, thoroughly unremorseful, and some twenty thousand dollars ahead of the game. She returned most of my money, I *think*. I'm not sure, since I don't know exactly how much she got away with. Anyway, I declined to prosecute, and she was still in Vegas the last I heard.

Still drunk, still unremorseful, and still a big winner.

32

I went to the hospital a few days after the Bannermans and Manny's husband tried to kill me. My house needed repairs to make it livable, and it was kind of lonesome there by myself, so I went to the hospital. And I remained there while the courts dealt with my would-be killers, and certain other happy events came to pass.

The doctors hinted that I was malingering and suggested that I do it elsewhere. Jeff Claggett gave me a stern scolding.

"You don't want to marry Nolton. You *shouldn't* marry her. Why not lay it on the line with her, instead of pulling the sick act?"

"Well . . . I do like her, Jeff," I said. "And she saved my life, you know."

"Oh, hell! She was goofing off when she should have been on the job, and we both know it."

"Well . . . but I promised to marry her. I didn't think I'd ever be free of Connie at the time, but—"

"That wasn't a promise, dammit! Anyway, you've

got a right to change your mind. You shouldn't go ahead with something that's all wrong to keep a promise that should never have been made."

"I'm sure you're right," I said. "I'll have a talk with Kay as soon as I get some other things out of the way."

"What things?"

"Well . . ."

"You've got a go-ahead on your erosion book and a hefty advance from the publisher. You're getting a good settlement on your condemnation suit; my lawyer friend says it will be coming through any day now. So what the hell are you waiting for?"

"Nothing," I said firmly. "And I won't wait any longer."

"Good! You'll settle with Nolton right away, then?"

"You bet I will," I said. "Maybe not right away, but . . ."

He cursed, and stamped out of the room.

The phone rang, and of course it was Kay.

"Just one question, Britt Rainstar," she said. "How much longer do you plan on staying in that hospital?"

"What's the difference?" I said. "My divorce hasn't come through yet."

"Hasn't it?" she said. "Hasn't it?"

"I, uh, well—" I laughed nervously. "I haven't received the papers yet, but I believe I did hear that, uh— My goodness, Kay," I said, "you surely don't think that I don't want to marry you."

"That's exactly what I think, Britt."

"Well, shame on you," I said. "The very idea!"

"Then, when are you leaving the hospital?"

"Very soon," I said. "Practically any day now."
She slammed down the phone.
I lay back on the pillows and closed my eyes.

I was thoroughly ashamed of myself. My shame increased as the days drifted by and I stayed on in the hospital. The naive, evasive-child manner I maintained was evidence of my general feeling of hopeless unworthiness. The I-ain't-nothin'-but-a-hound-dawg routine set to different music.

Whatever I did, I was bound to make someone unhappy, and I have always shrunk from doing that. I am always terribly unhappy when I make others unhappy.

I wondered what in the name of God I could tell Manny. After all, I had told her that the only reason I didn't marry her was because I couldn't. I was married to Connie, and there was no way I could dissolve our marriage. Now, however, I was free of Connie, and Manny was free of her husband. So how could I possibly tell her that I was marrying Kay Nolton?

I was wrestling with the riddle the afternoon she came to see me, the first time I had seen her since that seemingly long-ago day when she had come to the house.

I stalled on giving her the news about Kay, staving it off by complimenting her on how nice she looked. She thanked me and said she certainly hoped she looked nice.

"You see, I'm getting married, Britt," she said. "I thought you should be the first to know."

I gulped and said, "Oh," thinking that that took me

off the hook all right—or sank it into me. "Well, I hope you'll be very happy, Manny."

"Thank you," she said. "I'm sure I will be."

"Is it, uh, anyone I know?"

"We-el, no. . . ." She shook her head. "I don't believe you do. You're going to get acquainted with him, because I intend to see that you do. And I think you'll like him—the real *him*—a lot better than the man you think you know."

"Uh, what?" I frowned. "I don't understand."

"Well, you'd just better!" Her voice rose, broke into joyous laughter. "You'd better, you nutty, mixed-up mixed-blood, or I'll take your pretty gray-streaked scalp!"

She came to me at a run, flung herself down on the bed with me.

Naturally, the bed collapsed noisily.

We were picking ourselves up when the door slammed open and a nurse came rushing in. She had red hair and beautiful long legs and a scrubbed-clean look.

"Kay—," I stammered. "W-what are you doing here?"

She snapped that her name was Nolton, *Miss* Nolton, and she was there because she was a nurse, as I very well knew. "Now, what's going on here, Miss?" she demanded, glaring at Manny. "Never mind! I want you out of here, right this minute! And for goodness sake—*for goodness sake*—do us all a favor and take him with you!"

"Oh, I intend to," Manny said sunnily. "I'm getting married, and he's the bridegroom."

"Well, I'm glad to hear it," Kay said. "I'm g-glad that s-someone's willing to marry him. He had t-that—that I—"

She turned suddenly, and hurried out the door.

Manny came into my arms, and I did what you do when a very lovely girl comes into your arms. And then, over her shoulder, I saw the door ease open. And I saw that it was Kay who had opened it.

She stuck out her tongue at me.

She winked and grinned at me. And, then, just as she closed the door, she turned on a truly beautiful blush.

And when it comes time to close the door on someone or something, I know of no nicer way to do it.

Subscription to THE NEW BLACK MASK
$27.80/year in the U.S.

Subscription correspondence should be sent to
THE NEW BLACK MASK
129 West 56th Street
New York, NY 10019